14.77

JAY VERSUS THE SAXOPHONE OF DOOM

JAY VERSUS THE SAXOPHONE OF DOOM

KARA KOOTSTRA

WITH ILLUSTRATIONS BY KIM SMITH
AND AN AFTERWORD BY BOBBY ORR

PUFFIN

an imprint of Penguin Canada Books Inc., a Penguin Random House Company

Published by the Penguin Group

Penguin Canada Books Inc., 320 Front Street West, Suite 1400, Toronto, Ontario M5V 3B6, Canada

Penguin Group (USA) LLC, 375 Hudson Street, New York, New York 10014, U.S.A.

Penguin Books Ltd, 80 Strand, London WC2R 0RL, England

Penguin Ireland, 25 St Stephen's Green, Dublin 2, Ireland (a division of Penguin Books Ltd)

Penguin Group (Australia), 707 Collins Street, Melbourne, Victoria 3008, Australia

(a division of Pearson Australia Group Pty Ltd)

Penguin Books India Pvt Ltd, 11 Community Centre, Panchsheel Park, New Delhi—110 017, India

Penguin Group (NZ), 67 Apollo Drive, Rosedale, Auckland 0632, New Zealand

(a division of Pearson New Zealand Ltd)

Penguin Books (South Africa) (Pty) Ltd, 24 Sturdee Avenue, Rosebank, Johannesburg 2196, South Africa

Penguin Books Ltd, Registered Offices: 80 Strand, London WC2R 0RL, England

First published 2017

1 2 3 4 5 6 7 8 9 10   (RRD)

Text copyright © Kara Kootstra, 2017
Illustrations copyright © Kim Smith, 2017
Afterword copyright © Bobby Orr, 2017

Manufactured in the U.S.A.

Library and Archives Canada Cataloguing in Publication

Kootstra, Kara, 1982–, author
Jay versus the saxophone of doom /
Kara Kootstra ; illustrated by Kim Smith.

Issued in print and electronic formats.
ISBN 978-0-670-06940-8 (hardcover).—ISBN 978-0-14-319374-6 (paperback).
—ISBN 978-0-14-319375-3 (epub)

I. Smith, Kim, 1986–, illustrator II. Title.
PS8621.O665B69 2017   jC813'.6   C2016-900945-9
                                                   C2016-900946-7

Visit the Penguin Canada website at www.penguinrandomhouse.ca

MAR 2 3 201  Penguin
Random
House

For two great encouragers of my creativity—
Lynne and Pam

CHAPTER 1

Three beeps.

Three, long, ear-piercingly loud, ANNOYING beeps.

Three beeps that sound to my foggy, half-awake brain a whole lot like, "Get up, Jay, it's the first day of school, and another fun-filled year of torturous misery awaits you!"

My eyes still closed, I feel around the nightstand until my hand finally reaches the top of the terrible plastic thing. I smack the button a couple of times before the blaring stops, and let out a small yawn as I finally crawl out of bed. Quickly throwing on my T-shirt and jeans, it occurs to me that getting ready for the first day of school isn't all that different from getting ready for a hockey game. Put on the right uniform. Pack the right gear. Eat a good breakfast (well, that's what my mom says, anyway, and if I try to leave without eating she basically pries my mouth open and shoves the food in).

Keep your eyes open. Watch your opponents. Most kids just play by the rules and the game is easy. Maybe if I could bring a stick and a pair of skates to school I would find it easy too.

GAME TIP #1: *Do not bring a hockey stick to school, as it is considered a weapon and you will be sent to the principal's office. I won't get into it, but trust me on this one.*

It's not that school is completely terrible. I've always managed to do all right, and there are a few subjects that I even kind of like. But that doesn't mean I'm the guy skipping to school, excitedly waiting to do a math problem, either. I mean, I guess I'm not really the guy that "skips" anywhere, but my point is I am DEFINITELY not skipping to school. Here's the thing. Sometimes when I'm in class my mind tends to wander a bit. And it usually wanders to one particular subject. In fact, I'm thinking about it right now. The greatest game in existence. (You didn't think football, did you? Tell me you didn't think football.) It is, of course, HOCKEY. You could say I'm a little obsessed.

The other problem with school is that I am constantly trying to avoid MICK BARTLET. Mick is a very large, VERY annoying kid who has been in the same class as me literally every year since kindergarten. He's always calling me "squirt" (I'm not the biggest kid around) and he takes great pleasure in trying to ruin my life. My mom always says that I'm being "dramatic" when I say things like that, but I swear the guy has "Ruin Jay's Life" on a checklist somewhere. I guess the word to describe Mick would be "bully," although he has never tried to take my lunch money or anything. Bullies in the movies usually do that.

Maybe this will finally be the year that Mick is put in a different class. The odds have to work in my favor eventually, right? Right.

Now, if my mom were here right now, she would probably say that I'm being rude because I haven't introduced myself. She would also probably tell me to "Get that hair out of your eyes so I can see your handsome face," or "For goodness sake, Jason, you're going to bite your nails right down to the bone," or my personal favorite, "Take your elbows off the table, this is not a horse's stable!" But I suppose an introduction is probably in order.

My name is Jason, but most people just call me Jay or J.R. or Roberts, which is my last name. You should also know that on occasion my friends call me "Ralph" (which, in case you weren't aware, is another word for vomit), referring to an incident at camp involving a whole bag of marshmallows and a shaken can of pop. I will spare you the details of that tragic night, in case you have a weak stomach or you started reading this book right before breakfast.

Okay, this is starting to feel like one of those "All About Me" assignments we used to do in school. You know, the one where you have to fill a whole page about what you like to do and then finish it off with a picture of yourself, which doesn't look anything like you because for some reason every kid draws a self-portrait without a neck or, like, ankles or something. I used to do pretty poorly on those things because not only was my picture neck-lacking but also I don't really have a whole lot of different things I like to do. In fact, I only have one thing I like to do, as I've already mentioned.

Hockey.

But we'll get back to that. I should probably tell you a little bit about my family, or maybe the correct expression is *warn* you about my family, as they are all pretty weird and I am just about the only normal person that lives in this house. Don't believe me? Here's the lineup.

JODIE

Jodie is my older sister, and she thinks she is SO UNBELIEVABLY COOL because she's in her second year of high school. I think it is SO UNBELIEVABLY COOL that I only have to wait three years before she goes away to university. Jodie moving out will mean two things for me. First of all, I will get her room, which is substantially bigger than mine. Second of all, I will no longer have to deal with her excessive eye-rolling.

Mom: "What happened at school today?"

Eye-roll.

Dad: "Do you want to go to the movies tonight?"

Eye-roll.

Me: "Would you like a brand-new car, a million dollars, and a private island named after you?"

You got it: eye-roll.

Jodie pretty much lives to torture me, and since you probably think I'm exaggerating, let me tell you a quick story. When I was six, I had an imaginary friend named Zach. (Oh, come on, I was six . . . as if you didn't have an imaginary friend when you were little. You're probably picturing him right now.) Anyway, Zach was the coolest imaginary friend ever. Among other things, he could fly and shoot laser beams out of his fingers. I mean, if you're going to make up a friend, you might as well make him AWESOME, right? So one day, I come home from school and Jodie sits me down to tell me that Zach was involved in a terrible accident and, tragically, his injuries were fatal.

Yes, that's right. My sister KILLED MY IMAGINARY FRIEND. Now, in hindsight, I should have realized that no one can kill a person who isn't real, but at the time I was inconsolable. So, in order to "help" her grief-stricken brother, my sister planned a funeral for Zach. Yep, the first funeral I ever attended was for my imaginary friend. My sister played a song on her recorder and I made a speech and everything. Pretty twisted, right? And think . . . I sleep right down the hallway from her.

DYLAN

Dylan is two years older than me and is in grade eight. We have kind of a love-hate relationship. One day we're playing video games or pickup hockey with kids on our street, and the next day he's hiding my helmet an hour before a playoff game. (Side note: I did end up finding the helmet, which had been dipped in water and hidden in our freezer. Dylan thought it was pretty funny, until I returned the favor with his jock-strap.) Dylan just pretends I don't exist when we see each other at school, unless he needs to mooch off my lunch because he forgot his. This arrangement suits me just fine.

DAD

My dad is your typical dad. He spends most of his days thinking of new and exciting ways to completely embarrass me. To date, he has an excellent track record. For example:

1. Insisting that a middle-aged man can totally "rock the hipster look." No, Dad, a father of three should definitely NOT be wearing skinny jeans.

2. Dropping me off at school and then rolling down the window to shout, "Jason, don't forget your doctor's appointment after school so that we can get that rash looked at," in front of everyone. Because he couldn't have remembered to say that five minutes ago when we were still in the car.

3. Singing along to the radio at the top of his lungs while we're carpooling my friends. Occasionally, this is accompanied by his version of "dance moves," which is really just a lot of body flailing, with a few fist-pumps thrown in.

MOM

My mom is what you would call a loud-talker. Most of the time, I'm so used to her piercingly loud voice that I don't even notice it. But then we'll be in a packed movie theater, and she'll "whisper" things like, "I don't get it . . . which one is the bad guy?" or "Oh, he's that actor from that other film . . . what was that film, dear? The one with the people from the future? You know the one, what was that called . . . ?" And you try to sink as low as you can into your seat and hope that people think you just happen to be seated next to the weird lady. Which usually doesn't work because she inevitably tries to pass you popcorn in a completely inappropriate, LOUD way.

And it's not just in movie theaters. She is loud in just about every social situation. For instance, Mom can't just go up to the check-in window at the doctor's office and discreetly let them know that her son is in to get a rash looked at. No, she needs to let the entire waiting room know where the rash is and how I can't stop scratching it. (Yes, I'm a little bitter about the rash situation. Mom and Dad both really let me down on that one.)

You see what I'm dealing with? I'm not saying they don't have their good qualities, but . . . it's kind of a madhouse around here.

And then there is the honorary member of my family. I can't possibly finish this "All About Me" introduction without mentioning my role model. My hero. THE BEST HOCKEY PLAYER TO EVER STEP ON THE ICE. (That's not an opinion—that's just a fact.) The one, the only . . .

BOBBY ORR

Living in Parry Sound, the town where Bobby Orr was born, is definitely one of the reasons I grew up knowing about him, but it was my Grandpa Joe who passed on his love for hockey and his Bobby Orr super-fan status to my father and me. I can still remember sitting with my grandpa in his old corduroy chair, poring over highlights from Bobby Orr's career (which was much too short—"a crying shame," Grandpa would say). Grandpa would be munching on pretzels, giving his own commentary over the announcer's. I couldn't believe the stuff that Bobby Orr could do on the ice— easily skating around his opponents to find his way to the net for a goal, or, if his team was unable to score, fading back to play his position as a defenseman. I knew that, just like my grandpa, I would be a fan for life.

In fact, my whole family loves Bobby Orr and his old team, the Boston Bruins. Watching a Bruins game is literally still the ONE thing we can all do together that doesn't end in some form of yelling/hitting/crying, which I know would make my grandpa happy. A few years ago, Grandpa Joe passed away, leaving me with a ton of Bobby Orr memorabilia—hockey cards, jerseys, books, posters, even a bobblehead Bobby (try saying that five times fast). Dad says that even though Grandpa is gone, his love for the game and for his hero lives on in us.

But enough of that sappy stuff. Back to my original point: Bobby Orr is an honorary member of my family. Often, if I'm in a jam, on or off the ice, I try to imagine what the great Bobby Orr would do and go from there. (You might be thinking that it sounds like I still have an imaginary friend, but this is different. Mostly because there are no laser-hands involved. Although thinking about Bobby Orr with laser-hands is kind of an awesome visual.) I figure if I follow in Bobby Orr's footsteps then I will also become a PROFESSIONAL HOCKEY

PLAYER STANLEY CUP CHAMPION LEAD GOAL-SCORING DEFENSEMAN. Or . . . maybe something close to that, at least. And, of course, there is only one number I wear on the ice. The number of my hockey legend:

I play for a team called the Parry Sound Shamrocks (the same team Bobby Orr played for as a kid, no big deal) and I play center. Our season is just starting and we will soon be playing Saturday games with teams from neighboring towns. Our team is pretty solid so we usually do well, and I'm not trying to brag or anything but I can hold my own. I'm not the biggest or fastest guy out there, and it's not like I score a million goals a game or anything, but Dad says that I play the game "smart," meaning that I'm usually thinking a step ahead of the other guys. I can kind of see the play before it happens and get to where I need to be. And I can handle a puck, too, mostly because if I'm not in school or sleeping . . . I've got a stick in my hands and a puck at the end of it.

"Jay, sweetie, you're going to be late," my mother is shouting from the bottom of the stairs, her voice snapping me back to reality.

SCHOOL. I am almost 100 percent sure that our parents and/or teachers are involved in a conspiracy that is making every summer just a bit shorter. I can't prove it yet, but I had barely put on my board shorts when my mom was dragging me to the mall for back-to-school shopping.

Last year, my teacher taught me what the word "synonym" means. A synonym is a word that means the same thing as another word. Like *couch* and *sofa*. Or *wrong* and *incorrect*. So let me give you some synonyms for back-to-school shopping. Horrible-torture. Terrifying-nightmare. THE-WORST-THING-I-CAN-POSSIBLY-THINK-OF. (Okay, so, you get the point.) And here I am now, in the back-to-school clothes that my mom and I finally agreed on: a pair of jeans and a "presentable" T-shirt. Here is a list of the shirts that were not considered "presentable":

1. Shirts that look "faded." ("Honestly, Jason, nineteen dollars for a shirt that looks like someone poured bleach in the prewash cycle!?")
2. Shirts with phrases on them. ("What does *pwnd* mean? There isn't even a vowel in it.")
3. Black shirts. ("They look depressing.")
4. White shirts. ("They stain too easily.")
5. Any shirts that will make someone look—in any way, shape, or form—cool.

So I am wearing a plain, pale blue t-shirt, because, let's face it, that's way better than the dress shirt tucked into a pair of khakis that my mom thought looked "dashing and smart." After all, I'm just a kid trying to survive the sixth grade.

Give a guy a chance.

CHAPTER 2

I kinda-sorta make my bed by throwing the covers up near the pillow region, then I look at the clock: 8:15. Gotta go. I shove all my newly purchased school supplies into my backpack and head down the stairs, already anticipating the scene that is awaiting me.

Here's the play-by-play:

GAME TIP #2: *Never EVER let your mom convince you to take a photo with a prop. It doesn't matter what the prop is . . . a book, an apple, even something you think is cool. You will always end up looking lame, and you will have to walk by that picture in the hallway for the rest of your life every time you go to the bathroom.*

"Oh, Jay, darling! You look so handsome!"

I can tell my mother is already getting weepy so I quickly sit down and ask my dad to pass the cereal, hoping to avert a messy-crying-crazy-emotional situation. When I actually start to pour my favorite cereal into the bowl, only a few tiny pieces fall out of the box, which causes Dylan to break out into hysterical laughter (a total overreaction considering a five-year-old wouldn't find this funny) as he shovels heaping spoonfuls of the stuff into his mouth. Dylan doesn't even like cereal.

"Honestly, Dylan, you are so immature," Jodie says, and she demonstrates her award-winning eye-roll.

"That's all right, Jay. Have a piece of toast." My dad starts to pass me a piece of his marmalade-slathered breakfast but I am able to cut him off in time (I feel I need to say this again, MARMALADE IS GROSS).

"It's okay, Dad. I think I'm just going to toast a bagel."

Dylan is still snickering, so I shoot him an unimpressed look and he responds with an innocent shrug. I stick half a bagel into the toaster and open the fridge, only to find that there is no cream cheese. No cereal. No cream cheese. This is beginning to feel like a bad omen for the first day of school. Letting out a frustrated sigh, I pull out the jar of peanut butter and wait for the bagel to toast. I try to remember if I have everything I need for school, but my thoughts are disrupted when my dad starts talking excitedly in between marmalade-toast bites.

"... and this guy says to me—well, this kid, I should say, couldn't have been more than sixteen years old— he says to me, 'Maps are kind of ... like ... old school.' So I tell him, he's darn right they're old school. Old school and reliable. I'm telling you, all this GPS gadgetry, it all runs on batteries that have to be charged. Charged! And what happens if there is some kind of energy crisis? I'll tell you what happens. Everyone will be coming to see old Jon Roberts to get a map. Old school! You bet I'm old school ..." Dad continues, only now he's just talking under his breath (or perhaps the correct term is mumbling), while my mom smiles and nods, listening to yet another map rant.

My dad has always had what I would describe as an unhealthy map obsession, which led to him quitting his job as an insurance salesman to open his very own map store three years ago. Let me be honest with you. I might have thrown around the words "terrible" and "crazy" and "the worst idea ever" when Dad first talked about opening a store in downtown Parry Sound. Our downtown is not exactly "booming with business," and a lot of shops have had to close because of bigger stores being built just outside of town. But every summer, my dad's store gets a rush of cottagers and campers making their way through Parry Sound, and when my mom isn't working at the dentist's office, she helps him run an online division of his business. Apparently maps are, like, some kind of decorating thing now? So I guess, in a way, some people might actually consider my dad "trendy." (I am not one of those people.)

To be honest, I really enjoy going into my dad's shop. Sometimes I stop by after school if I don't have practice and thumb through the pages of a huge atlas, or spin one of the globes super fast and stop it with my finger, pretending that spot will be my next travel destination. (If I land on Antarctica I get a free spin because, well . . . it's Antarctica.) The shop always has this new-paper smell that I love, and Dad keeps a small dish of candy by the cash register that I am allowed to take from, "within reason" my mom says. Plus, the store is always pretty empty so I can do my homework there in peace and quiet, which is often impossible at home with my family.

I finish the rest of my bagel and quickly half-smile for the pictures I will soon come to regret (my mom tossed me a pile of books before I could realize they were props), just as Luke is walking through my front gate.

His backpack is slung over his shoulder, half open, and he motions through the window for me to hurry up. Luke Benson lives six houses down from me, plays on the Shamrocks, and has been my best friend since kindergarten. To say the two of us look different would be what my mother refers to as "an understatement." Luke is huge, with dark, curly hair that people refer to as "the beast." Me, I'm a bit on the smaller side ("scrawny," according to Jodie) with a short haircut that is too boring for a nickname. On occasion I have actually been mistaken for Luke's little brother, and my so-called "best friend" does nothing to correct this mistake. In fact, he gets a strangely satisfied smile on his face and usually replies with something like, "Yeah, I've got to keep an eye on this little guy, he's always running off!" Thanks, Luke. Really appreciate that. But it's all good. As different as we look on the outside, at any given time he's thinking exactly the same thing I am:

Is there a hockey game on tonight? When's our next hockey practice? Hockey, hockey, other stuff . . . hockey, hockey, hockey, pointless stuff . . . hockey.

So, yeah. We get along pretty well.

I finally manage to duck out of the house, safe. At least I think I am.

"Hey, looks like your mom wants you." Luke is grinning and pointing behind me at my mother, who is frantically waving from my front door. I turn and give her a small wave back, fearing that the waving will lead to yelling and/or hugging if I don't respond. I turn back to Luke, who is still grinning, and give him a friendly punch on the arm.

"Do I really need to bring up the note from your lunch last year?" I put on my best mom voice. "*Dear Lukey. Do not trade your cookies for pudding cups. You know what pudding cups do to you—*"

"All right, all right," Luke interrupts, punching me back. "Point taken."

I push open our old metal gate, wiping the bits of rusty black paint off my coat before slamming it shut. It isn't a very long walk to school, but when you live in a place like Parry Sound, population 6,200, most things are pretty close, which is great. Living in a small town is not without its disadvantages, though. I mean, besides the movie theater and the mall (and I refer to it as a "mall" in the loosest sense of the term), there isn't much going on around town most of the time. However, Parry Sound is the home of the Bobby Orr Hall of Fame (I may have visited it a few . . . hundred times), and it does sit right beside Georgian Bay, which is part of Lake Huron. And that means . . .

Pond hockey.

Playing hockey on an indoor rink is great, but there is something amazing about a mid-February game on the frozen bay, often with most of the kids from the neighborhood, sometimes with just a few. It doesn't really matter how many people play. There aren't any real nets, just some pieces of old wood or a pair of boots, a couple of markers that the puck needs to slide between to count as a goal. The feel of the ice is different, and you can almost hear a cracking sound as your blades make contact with the frozen surface. When the wind is at your back it can seem as though you are gliding, downhill, barely needing to exert energy to make your legs move toward your goal. When it's coming at you, it's as though imaginary hands are pushing you backwards, causing you to fight hard for every inch up the ice. But no matter what the conditions are outside, and I don't have any scientific data to back this up, it always seems like I can skate faster on an outdoor rink. Go figure.

When you're out on the bay, the only rules are your rules. We are the coaches, the referees, and the players, and aside from an occasional argument, the games go off without a hitch. Sometimes we play until dark, and sometimes even later, if Mark's dad brings the lights from his construction site. My mom doesn't understand how we can play all day without freezing, but you don't always feel the cold when you are skating from one end of the "rink" to the other. We'll worry about the cold later. Can I feel my toes? No. But I am fairly certain they are still there, and the fact is, when I'm out on the ice, nothing else matters, and I don't want it to end. When the game is finished, well, that's another story. Suddenly the cold creeps in, and we run home quickly, hoping our moms will heat up a bit of hot chocolate to warm our hands and our insides. When you finally climb into bed and pull the covers up, it only takes a few seconds to fall fast asleep.

We may only have five stores in our mall, but having that big "pond" right there makes it all worth it.

The road I live on in our little town is narrow, dotted with tiny, old houses all snuggled close together. I know most of the people on our street, and as Luke and I pass by on our way to school, most of the neighbors nod or wave, unless they are preoccupied with their outdoor chores.

GAME TIP #3: *DO NOT start a conversation with someone who is trimming their lawn, by hand, with scissors. You will end up on their porch listening to how things were in the "good old days" and how "kids these days" just don't know about a hard day's work. You may also be served and expected to eat stale maple-flavored cookies.*

When we get to school, Luke and I slip into our classroom just as the final morning bell rings. We choose the same seats every year, in the back row, right next to each other. Our homeroom teacher's name is Mrs. Vanderson, and it just so happens that she was our homeroom teacher last year.

"It's so nice to have you all back," Mrs. Vanderson says, snapping a few pages into her clipboard. "I hope you all had a wonderful summer and are ready to start a new year of learning!"

Luke turns to me and rolls his eyes, but I don't respond. Mrs. Vanderson is the best teacher I've ever had, even if she is a little, well, excitable when it comes to school. I quickly scan the room, not believing my eyes. Is it possible? Could it really be true? Have I managed to be put in a class that is free from Mick Bar—?

"Sorry I'm late, miss."

I look up to see Mick Bartlet at the classroom door quickly making his way toward a desk. Annnnnnd . . . my unlucky streak continues.

"Let's not make this a habit, Mr. Bartlet. All right, we're going to take attendance and then we'll look at our classroom rotation schedule for the year. When I call your name, please raise your hand and say 'Here' in a nice, loud voice."

She calls through the entire list, and then Mrs. Vanderson asks if there is someone who would like to take the attendance to the office. I raise my hand quickly, but a girl, Sarah, beats me to the punch. I know taking the attendance to the office is only a five-minute job, but I will take five minutes out of class ANY day.

GAME TIP #4: *When you get the chance to bring the attendance to the office, your teacher does not tell you which ROUTE you have to take. I have devised a series of turns on my path to the office that extends my time out of class by 2.5 minutes. Worth it? Absolutely.*

"Okay, I'm going to hand out the classroom schedules, so just take one and pass it on."

Mrs. Vanderson places a stack of papers on the first desk of the front row.

"Now, I expect everyone to be following along as we all go through this information together. Our first class on Day 1 will be Math, so that means no one will be able to fill in their math homework over the lunch hour . . . I think you all know who I'm talking about." Mrs. Vanderson raises her eyebrows and a few kids in the class giggle. Chase is famous for asking everyone around him at lunch for answers to the math homework. He shrugs his shoulders and gives her an I-have-no-idea-what-you're-talking-about face.

"Let's see . . . moving on, you will have a full period of History, for which I will be assigning textbooks in just a moment. Be sure to write your name inside lightly in pencil, and remember that I expect them back in the same condition you received them."

I slink down a bit, wondering if she is referring to my Social Studies textbook from last year, which may or may not have had a few pages slightly damaged. But, I mean, no one ever told me not to put my open textbook in the bottom of a bag that also held skates with no guards on. It could have happened to anybody.

"Twice a week after History you will have a period of Music, which we will be extending to a full hour since you will be learning to play band instruments this year."

One hour. Music. Instruments.

My mouth instantly goes dry and my arms drop heavy at my sides. How could I have forgotten? Grade six is the year we have to choose and play musical instruments. *Musical instruments.* The words swirl around in my brain, and I realize that Mrs. Vanderson is still talking and I haven't heard a word she has said. I shake my head and try to focus.

". . . all be little Schuberts by the end of the year," Mrs. Vanderson is saying, and she finishes by clapping her hands together. What's this about *shoes?* And who is *Burt?* I am clearly losing it.

I look around to see if anyone else is sharing in my terror, but all the other kids seem to be following along with the schedule without a care in the world. Don't they know what happens in Music class? Every student is required to play a piece of music on their instrument in front of the WHOLE class. My brother had to learn the trumpet in the sixth grade and he told me all about it, probably with the intention of completely terrifying me.

It worked.

It's not that I can't take pressure. I mean, let's say there is a minute to go in the game, we're tied 3–3, and the puck comes my way. There's a good chance that story ends with me scoring the winning goal and the crowd going wild. But playing a music solo? In front of everybody? That's more likely to end up with me playing a song that is completely unrecognizable and the crowd throwing things at me.

And it's not that I don't like music. I just lack a few of the skills required to play it. Like rhythm. And pitch. And everything else that has to do with music.

EVIDENCE: My parents have a video of me in my very first school play. I was in grade one, and we had worked for months to prepare a musical presentation all about how the caterpillar turns into a (SPOILER ALERT) butterfly. Now, I realize that it is not expected that a seven-year-old is going to give a flawless performance in a grade-school play, but I was TERRIBLE. It is seriously hard to watch. I am completely out of time with all of the actions, and my squeaky, out-of-tune voice is clearly heard above everyone else's. (I was singing super loud because when you're seven you don't know you should be embarrassed yet.)

I feel dizzy. I fold my arms on the desk, put my head down, and close my eyes.

It's official. I, Jason Roberts, am doomed.

CHAPTER 3

There are some things in life that you just can't control. One of those things is your last name. I met this guy once who had the last name "Sucker." Unfortunate, right? I mean, what did this kid do to deserve the last name Sucker? Nothing. And it's worse when you're young. When he grows up, people might chuckle a bit when he signs his name, but in grade school? That's like walking around with a "Kick Me" sign on your back.

I suppose I was lucky that I didn't end up with a last name like Sucker. However, having "Roberts" is not without its disadvantages. Okay, let's do a little alphabet review.

The first letter of my last name is near the middle of the alphabet. Right? Wrong. Since I go to a small school in a small town, it just so happens that there aren't any kids with last names that start with *O* or *Q* or *U* or *V* or *W* or *X* or *Y* or *Z* so it really looks more like this.

Where does that leave me? One of the LAST kids on the attendance list. Do you know what the LAST kids on the attendance list get? They get everything LAST. And getting things LAST is about to really suck. Big time.

"You must dig deep, deep inside of your soul to find the music that is within, and then channel that through the instrument into the ears of your listeners."

I am sitting in my third-period Music class and Mrs. Jennings is standing at the front, giving us a music pep talk. (It is not making me feel peppy.) Mrs. Jennings is everything you would expect from a music teacher. She has long, blond, frizzy hair that drapes over a large collection of multicolored scarves tied around her neck. (It basically makes her looks like she has no neck. If I drew one of those "All About Me" assignments that featured Mrs. Jennings, I would totally nail it.) Her floor-length dress is made up of what looks like sewn-together patches, some with birds and some with flowers. At her waist, a kind of narrow, braided, rainbow belt is tied at one side, and the two ends spill down the length of her dress. There is so much color that—and I mean this—sometimes you literally have to squint your eyes a bit to adjust to the brightness. And then there are the bracelets. There must be a hundred of the heavy gold things on her wrists, so many that they make loud, clanking sounds every time she writes on the chalkboard or conducts the band with her little white stick. But if there is one thing that defines Mrs. Jennings, it's the way she walks. It's more like an energetic bound that makes you think she's always on a caffeine high, which might also explain why her eyes are perma-wide.

Okay, keep reading: here's when it happens.

"When I call your name, you can come to the front of the classroom and pick out your instrument. Remember, an instrument is not a toy, but a friend. A friend that must be treated with respect." Mrs. Jennings picks up a flute and gives it a small embrace, and I choose not to look over at Luke, who is without a doubt smirking in my direction. "All right, we'll start with Maggie Anderson."

I know who comes next. Mick Bartlet. Raymond Beacon. Luke Benson. Alissa Douglas. Hayden Ferguson. Everyone makes their way up to the front, picking up flutes and clarinets and trumpets. With each name called, the contents of the table shrink, until, finally, I am at the front, looking at three sad instruments, each with differing dents and scratches but with the same long, brassy hook shape.

"Well, it would appear the saxophone has chosen you, Mr. Roberts! It is one of the tougher instruments to play, but it is also one of the most soulful . . ." Her voice trails off and her eyes close, as if she is remembering something lovely.

Great. I have one of the tougher instruments to play. If only my last name were Adams or Anderson or Abram I could have picked the drum and had a fighting chance. But no, my fate has now officially been sealed. I pick up the saxophone (which seems to weigh about a hundred pounds) and trudge back to my seat. As I turn the hunk of metal over in my hands, I can almost swear the saxophone has a mouth. And, furthermore, it is wearing a very wide, very devilish grin.

By the time I sit down, the class has exploded with the sounds of kids laughing and making squeaks and blasts with their instruments. Somehow, Luke has managed to score a snare drum . . . the drum! I wonder how much allowance I would have to give him to switch with me. I catch his eye, and the mocking impression he is doing of someone playing the saxophone tells me I am out of luck.

My stomach makes a little gurgling sound, and I wonder if I am getting hungry for lunch or if it's responding to the nerves I feel just holding the saxophone in my hands. I take a closer look at the instrument, trying to figure out how I am supposed to use this weird-looking contraption to make music. On the top end, a small, black, curved part narrows almost to a point, presumably where my mouth goes. It has a strange silver band attached to it, and for a moment I wonder if it might be what holds the mouthpiece to the rest of the saxophone, but upon further inspection I decide that doesn't really make sense. My eyes move down to the mass of golden buttons, which appear sort of jumbled, like they are not in any kind of real order. I push a few of them for testing purposes. My fingers go down easily and I am surprised by how quickly I can switch from one button to the next. At least there is one thing I feel confident I can do . . . push buttons down really fast.

Here are a few other things I feel fairly confident I could do if tested:

- Eat an entire box of cookies.
- Draw stick people.
- School Luke on a video game.
- Imitate Jodie's eye-roll. (That didn't happen overnight, either. It has taken hard work and dedication.)

Why can't the big test be on that stuff?

I let out a sigh and turn my attention to the bottom of the instrument, which curves up into a horn shape. Looking into it, I notice a piece of chewing gum that another kid has obviously left from last year. Fantastic. I grab a piece of tissue from the front of the room and work on chipping the hardened substance from my saxophone, if only to delay actually trying to play the thing.

GAME TIP #5: *Parents will often say things that are not true to try and scare you out of doing something. Like telling you your face will get "stuck like that!" if you keep making a silly expression. Or if you don't eat your vegetables you will stop growing and stay kid-sized forever. But when your mom tells you not to fall asleep chewing gum . . . she's not kidding about that one.*

Okay. No matter how I feel about this, I am going to have to learn the saxophone in order to pass grade six Music, so I had better make my peace and get to it. If I can score in the last two minutes of the third period to tie up a game while killing a penalty, how hard could it be to make a few sounds out of a horn?

Here it goes. I am bringing the saxophone up to my mouth, I am blowing into the saxophone and—

"You need a reed, you know." Kaylee Gifford is looking at me as if I were sitting in my chair completely naked. With four arms. And a monkey in a clown suit on my shoulder.

"I need a what?" I try to shoot her back the same look, but I don't think it works.

"A *reed*?" Kaylee pulls out a thin rectangular something and hands it to me. "It makes the vibrations that cause sound to come out of the saxophone. It's the same thing with the clarinet." She points to her instrument, and then continues. "You put the reed in your mouth to wet it, like this." She stops talking to put the reed in her mouth. "And then you attach it right here." Kaylee unscrews that tiny silver part on her instrument, slides the reed in, and tightens the screws to hold it in place.

That's what the silver part is for! That was definitely going to be my second guess. Or maybe my third.

"But I'm sure you knew that." Kaylee smirks, and then plays a few notes on her clarinet. "I've been taking private clarinet lessons for years, so this class should be a breeze."

As I am trying to figure out how to slide the reed thingy in, it is dawning on me that I would actually rather be naked in class than have to learn the saxophone. And a couple of extra arms would come in handy. And, really, who doesn't want a monkey?

✖ ✖ ✖

The rest of the day goes by in a blur. Science. Social Studies. French. The only thing making this terrible day tolerable is the fact that I have hockey practice after school.

As soon as I walk in the door to my house, I run up the stairs, shove my new "friend" into a corner, and start packing my equipment bag. Practice jersey. Skates. Pads. Gloves. Helmet. I grab my stick and race back downstairs to meet Luke at the car. My dad's driving. We load everything in and are just getting buckled up when my dad turns up one of the "classics" so that he can make the drive to the rink as painful as possible.

You know when you try really hard not to think about something but it ends up being the only thing you can think of? For instance: It's Friday morning and you are going to see a movie after school that you have been WAITING AND WAITING to see. You try not to think of it. You do everything in your power to concentrate on something else. But what's the only thing you can think of while school drags on, slower than usual, sucking the very life right out of you? That's right. The movie. (Also the fact that at the movies you will be ordering a large popcorn with butter and then adding a bag of candy to it. That way, every once in awhile you go to grab a handful of popcorn and BAM . . . a delicious, sugary surprise! It's the only way to eat popcorn.) Well, that's how

I feel right now. But instead of looking forward to something, all I can think about is how much I'm dreading my musical "situation," and Dad's horrible radio station selection is not helping me forget my worries. In fact, it occurs to me, as my dad sings/screeches along to "Sweet Home Alabama," that it is most likely his fault that I am so terrible at music in the first place. Thanks for that, Dad. And as long as I'm thanking you for your genetic contributions, I also really appreciate the sticking-out ears and the awkwardly large middle toe.

GAME TIP #6: *Although it might seem like a good idea to just ask your dad to stop belting out "the oldies," doing so will actually only encourage him to sing louder and/or add dance moves. Just keep your head down and wait it out.*

Luckily, the rink isn't too far, and both Luke and I dive for the door handles as soon as we come to a complete stop. I hear my dad calling out "Where's the fire?" as we quickly grab our equipment bags, sling our skates over our shoulders, and head indoors. As soon as we are inside, I take a deep breath and instantly feel a sense of calm. I may not be able to make even the slightest squeak on that saxophone, but this . . . this I can do.

The dressing room is already full of my teammates, putting on equipment but mostly just messing around. I grab a seat on the bench and let the hum of the room drown out all of the thoughts running through my mind. The sound of tape ripping, wooden sticks being tossed onto the floor, a distant whistle from the ice. I unpack my equipment bag and then begin getting ready, already forgetting the troubles of the day. Everything slides on quickly—after all, I've done this routine a million times before.

Sometimes, when I'm getting ready for practice, I imagine what it would have been like for the real #4, Bobby Orr, to lace up his skates before heading out onto the ice. Did his dressing room look anything like mine? Did he feel nervous getting ready before a big game? *Were his thoughts preoccupied with the terror of having to play the saxophone?* Doubtful.

I finish lacing up my skates and turn to grab my stick before noticing it is not where I left it, leaning against the wall.

"Looking for this?" Mick Bartlet is standing in front of me holding my stick. I try to grab it but he jerks it away. "Look at that. Squirt here is slow on *and* off the ice." I hear laughter coming from Mick's gang, now assembling behind him.

Oh, did I forget to mention that not only do I have to deal with Mick at school but I've also had to play with him on the same hockey team since Novice? It has been *totally awesome* (and just in case it didn't come across, that was sarcasm). I can always count on him to try and ram me into the boards during a scrimmage, or pull some other kind of stunt. Like taking my stick.

"Hey Mick, c'mon . . . " I say, trying to sound nonchalant about the whole thing. "Practice is about to start, just give it back." I can see Luke getting up from his seat but I shake my head, signaling for him to stay out of this.

"Calm down, Squirt. I was just taking your stick to get it cut down. So that it's more, you know, your size?" Mick is laughing hysterically at his joke and he tosses my stick to one of his gang, who throws it across the room. "C'mon, guys, let's go." They make their way to the door, laughing as they exit the dressing room.

I walk across the room and pick up my stick, easily identifiable by the single strip of black tape in the middle of the blade, a little something I do in honor of my hero. Luke is beside me but we don't say a word to each other. We just make our way out of the dressing room and onto the ice.

I tighten my grip on the stick. *Okay, Mick Bartlet. Here comes #4.*

CHAPTER 4

My blades hit the ice and I begin to warm up, trying to focus my attention on getting loose and ignoring Mick and the rest of his crew, who are still laughing at the opposite end of the ice. I shoot a few pucks at the empty net, nothing too fast or fancy, just easing my way into practice. Coach blows his whistle and tells us to take a knee.

"All right, gentlemen, we're going to start with some battle-drills today. Let's get set up for Machine Gun."

We're starting with the Machine Gun drill? Apparently it is going to be *one of those* practices. What Coach refers to as "battle-drills" are a set of on-ice challenges designed to put us in pressure situations and possibly FREAK US OUT. Because it's one thing to skate with a puck around an orange cone, but something altogether different when someone puts a stick on you, or a shoulder into you. That's when you see who can play.

If Coach really wanted to put me in a pressure situation, he should have considered having some skating or shooting drills that include a saxophone. But let's not give the guy any new and terrifying ideas.

Okay, so this is the Machine Gun drill.

It isn't merely a one-on-one drill, or even a two-on-one drill. This is a *three-on-one* drill. You've got one person in front of the net who has thirty seconds to try to shoot as many pucks toward the goal as he possibly can. The problem? That would be the three guys between the shooter and the goal, doing everything they can to stop him. The three defenders can't use their sticks during the drill, so they only have two ways to achieve their objective—block any shot taken, or hunt down the shooter and make contact. It's fast. It's physical. It's exactly the type of drill I am not feeling up to at this precise moment. It looks like this:

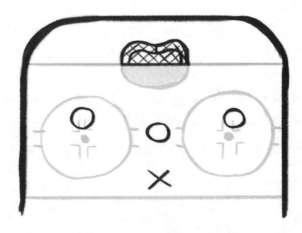

"Roberts?" My coach is pointing to a bucket beside the boards. "Grab the pucks from over there, dump 'em out on the ice, and take your place in front of the net. Bartlet, Smith, and Richards—you know what to do."

Perfect. I get to start out as the shooter. Well, so much for "easing" my way into practice. I grab the bucket and skate over in front of the net as instructed.

"Don't worry, Squirt. I'll take it easy on you. I only pick on people my own size. I wouldn't want to really hurt you," Mick says, stretching his arms from side to side.

I pretend that I don't hear him and turn the bucket upside down to drop the pucks onto the ice so they fall in a random pattern in front of the net.

"Everyone ready?" Coach already has his whistle in his mouth, and with a nod from each of us participating in the drill, he gives it a short blast.

I immediately start firing the pucks toward the net as quickly as I can, with the three defenders coming toward me at the same time. The first two pucks are just wide of the goal, but the third one whizzes in. I take another shot but hear a crack as it bounces off Smith's shin pad and sails in the opposite direction. The next one is blocked by Richards's skate, and then one hits the post. I keep shooting, one puck after another, all the while trying to dart and avoid the three guys coming at me. Some of my shots end up in the net, others near it, but most of them are blocked by the defenders. It's thirty seconds of insanity.

Mick has managed to do the majority of the blocking (not to mention some holding, clutching, and grabbing), and as the whistle blows again, signaling us to stop, he skates over to me and shoves me, saying, "C'mon, give me a challenge!"

Practice continues with more of Coach's battle-drills, followed by some conditioning work. He finishes things off with a short game of half-ice four-on-four. By the time we're done, I am drenched in sweat, ridiculously tired, and happy to see my dad's car already waiting in the parking lot. I am definitely ready to have this day OVER.

Dad asks us about practice on the way home and I try to engage in small talk, but Luke realizes I am not in the mood for conversation and answers most of the questions. When I get home he has already messaged me.

Jay you there

Yep

I can almost hear my mom: "I don't understand it. Whatever happened to proper punctuation? And since when did 'yep' become a full sentence?"

mick was being dumb

just doing it because he knows you can
smoke him on the ice 👊

i know

not upset about that

?????

(See, Mom? We totally use punctuation.)

sax.

you're going to get all the ladies

not funny

chill

can't you just get a tutor?

i got one for math

A tutor! Why didn't I think of that? Luke, you're a
genius! You're a godsend! You're . . .

k bye

I turn off my computer and start getting ready for
bed. A tutor, of course! It's not as if I am unteachable . . .
I just haven't ever really given it a shot before. I will
get a tutor. And in a few days, a couple of weeks at the
most, playing the saxophone will be as easy as skating.
I close my eyes, and for the first time since Music class,

the huge knot in my stomach is gone and I can breathe easy once again.

× × ×

There are 58 seconds on the clock.

I'm not sure where the puck came from, but somehow it's now on my stick blade. I start to skate up the ice, but my legs feel heavy, and it takes all of my strength just to weave around my opponents. I look up to see if one of my teammates is near the net, waiting for a pass, but no one's there. Why can't I move faster? I will myself to keep going, to keep possession of the puck. There's the net. C'mon, Jay. Everyone is watching. It's all on you. Just get the puck in the net. I pull back my stick, but something about it feels wrong. My hands are not gripping the layered, worn-down tape that is usually there. Instead, I feel the distinct coolness of metal, and it sends a shiver down my spine. I bring my stick down, only to realize it is not a stick at all.

It's a saxophone.

"Play for us, Jason, dear!" Mrs. Jennings is in the net, wearing a full goalie uniform but still sporting her usual scarves and accessories. "Just a little tune? We're all waiting . . ."

All around me, I can hear people starting to chant: "Play! Play! Play!" I look up at the stands but all I can make out are dark shadows.

Mrs. Jennings is moving closer. "It's time to play, Jason. You need to play." I turn around to try to find one of my teammates but I am alone on the ice. "Jason? Jason!" Mrs. Jennings is almost in front of me now and getting closer with each passing second. "Jason! JASON!!! For goodness sake, Jason, do you really want to be late on the second day of school?"

My eyes pop open. A nightmare! It was all just a silly nightmare. My mom is picking up some clothes from the floor and asking if I think she's my maid. I give a quick apology, which seems to appease her, and she grabs a pile of my laundry on her way out the door. I have dealt with some pretty tough opponents on the ice, but trust me . . . none of them have anything on my mom when she's in a mood.

GAME TIP #7: *It's a good idea to learn the meaning of the word "rhetorical." When someone asks a "rhetorical" question, it means they are not expecting you to answer. So, when your mom makes a really bad meal (I mean, you're not even sure what's on your plate), and she says, "Oh, I suppose you would rather eat at Luke's house?" Yeah . . . she doesn't want an answer for that one. Pick up a fork and eat. Any inquiries relating to: the state of your room/your mom being a maid, bad marks on your report card, a hockey bag that has not been cleaned out for a week, the second hat that has gone missing at school, a last-minute project that you haven't brought up until the night before . . . all rhetorical questions.*

I take a quick shower, get dressed, and grab a piece of toast on my way out the door. I find Luke sitting on my front steps. He shoots me an unimpressed look, I assume because he has had to wait for me, and I mutter an excuse about not hearing my alarm. My mom wasn't kidding about the time, and Luke and I have to sprint across the playground just to make it in by the bell.

We take our seats just before Mrs. Vanderson instructs us to take out last night's Math homework. I pull out my binder and start flipping to find the correct page when a tiny, crumpled piece of paper lands on my desk. I turn to Luke, expecting that it came from him, but he's grabbing loose papers out of his backpack and seems concerned that he hasn't found the right one. Luke is good at math, much better than I am, but his organizational skills are a little lacking.

I unfold the paper and find a small cartoon that looks like this:

I immediately know that Mick is behind this, and I try not to give him the satisfaction of looking in his direction. Unfortunately, this is hard to do. Sitting at the back of the class may have a lot of advantages (you are picked on less to give homework answers; it's much easier to grab a quick nap when you are reading a really boring novel in English; you're right in front of the heating vents, which comes in handy when December rolls around), but the one disadvantage? I can see everyone, whether I want to or not. Mick is completely turned around in his chair, so it is only a matter of time before our eyes meet. He mouths the word "Squirt," whispers something to the kid next to him, and starts laughing. I turn to say something to Luke, who is still frantically searching through wrinkled papers, when suddenly I hear my name.

"Jason? Question three, please?"

I freeze and look down at my binder, turning the pages, trying to find the question I'm supposed to be answering.

"Perhaps next time you will follow along with the rest of the class. Christine, can you give us the answer for number three?"

I feel my face flushing and I sink back in my chair. Even though my eyes are pointed down at my desk, I sense that Mick is looking at me, laughing even, and it makes my face feel even hotter. The day is off to a rough start, and it's not even Music class yet.

In fact, it's not even nine o'clock.

✖ ✖ ✖

By the time Music rolls around I am feeling a bit better. Mostly because Mick got called on to answer a math problem and totally got it wrong. And then, at recess, one of the eighth-graders was dared to drink a whole can of soda in a minute, and he tried it but totally failed, and there was soda everywhere, and it even came out of his nose. It. Was. Awesome. Also, a new thought has occurred to me: What if it turns out I'm actually really good at the saxophone? I mean, I've never tried to play an instrument before. Maybe it will be like the first time I laced up a pair of skates and got on the ice. Kind of wobbly at first, sure, but after a while I'll get the hang of it. I might even be pretty good. For all I know, I'm some kind of musical prodigy! Okay, that might be taking it a bit far, but the point is that I might be making this out to be a lot worse than it is. Maybe it's all in my head!

I take my seat in the saxophone section (I'm not sure you can call three kids a section, but whatever) and open up my case. Last class, Mrs. Jennings helped us assemble our instruments, and now I realize that I should probably have been paying more attention to which part goes where. I look at the rest of the saxophone players putting their instruments together at a shockingly fast pace. What, are these kids doing saxophone speed drills at home? I try to copy them as best as I can. I'm feeling so good by the time it's finished (after all, it certainly *looks* like a saxophone) that I almost forget that I am going to have to *play* the saxophone. That is, until Mrs. Jennings taps her music stand and asks us all to turn to the first page of our music books.

"Now, in today's class, we are all going to try to play a concert C on our instruments. For some of you, that note will look like this," she draws a strange symbol on the board, "and for others, it will look like this," more circles and sticks. "So, we'll go through each instrument section, I'll give you the fingering, and we'll give it a try! Oh, can't you just feel the music inside of you, ready to burst out!" Mrs. Jennings claps her hands together a few times.

I don't feel music inside of me wanting to burst out. I feel lunch wanting to burst out. I try to calm my nerves and wait for my section to be called.

Clarinets. Trumpets. Flutes.

"And now, my brave saxophone players. Look at

your chart and find the fingering for concert C. Does everyone have it?"

I am desperately putting fingers on metal buttons, trying to make it match the chart.

"Okay, now I hope all of you moistened your reeds!"

Moistened my *what?* Oh, right, the little wooden thing. I quickly stick it in my mouth to give it some moisture, then fumble as I slide it into place underneath the metal part on the mouthpiece.

"And a 1, and a 2, and a 1, 2, 3, 4 . . ."

Tightening the small screws as fast as I can, I take a deep breath in on "4" and blow as hard as I can into the saxophone. An enormous, high-pitched squeak comes out of my instrument, and I almost fall out of my chair, the sound is so loud. The entire class is erupting with laughter while Mrs. Jennings is tapping furiously on her stand. For the second time that day, my face turns red.

"Class . . . class! We do not laugh at budding musicians, we applaud our classmate's effort! Come on, everyone, let's give a nice big round of applause!"

I can't decide if it is more embarrassing to have everyone laugh at my terrible, high-pitched squeak or have everyone clap for it.

At any rate, I think I can officially say I am NOT a musical prodigy. If you were to put this experience on a scoreboard, it would probably look a little something like this:

JAY   **SAXOPHONE**

CHAPTER 5

It is almost the end of November and the classroom is a little louder than normal, mostly because of the announcement that we will finally get to go outside during our lunch period. At the beginning of the week, Parry Sound suddenly got super cold and the teachers had to keep us inside for three days. It's a good thing it finally started to warm up because kids were kind of starting to climb the walls and most of the teachers looked like they were going to have some kind of a breakdown. Luke and Max (who is my other hockey-obsessed friend) are sitting at their desks and I plunk down beside them into my own, unzipping the top of my lunch box.

"Took you long enough," Luke says, taking what looks like a bunch of lettuce out of a Ziploc bag. "Did you walk home to get that or what?" He is peeling off the top leaf of the lettuce, which reveals a piece of ham and a thick spread of some description.

"I had to go the bathroom, and the ones by our lockers were closed because the floors were being cleaned, so—" I start to respond, but Max interjects, looking at Luke.

"I think the better question is, what the heck are you eating? Hasn't your mom ever heard of a *sandwich?*" Max picks up his own sandwich to show Luke.

"It *is* a sandwich," Luke explains, "it's just . . . made with lettuce," he finishes, a bit defensively.

"No, a sandwich, by definition, is two pieces of bread with something in the middle," Max says, taking a big bite out of his own and wiping his mouth with the sleeve of his shirt.

"That's totally not true. A sandwich is when you put something in the middle of two slices of something else. It doesn't have to be bread. Right, Ralph?"

I ignore the nickname and just hold my hands up to indicate I am staying out of this debate.

"Dude, that's ridiculous. Read a dictionary."

"Oh, so you've read the definition of a sandwich in the dictionary, huh?" Luke asks, giving him a doubtful look.

"I don't have to, everyone knows what a sandwich is. You are born with the knowledge. Like knowing that ice cream is delicious and sisters are terrible human beings."

"You were born an idiot," Luke says, grabbing the ham from the middle of the lettuce and shoving it into his mouth.

"After all that, you aren't even going to eat your so-called sandwich?" Max asks, finishing his last bite.

"I said it was a sandwich. I didn't say it was good," Luke responds, putting the lettuce back into the plastic baggie and rolling it up into a ball. He attempts to shoot it into the garbage pail by the teacher's desk, but it misses, landing a few inches beside the can. Max stands up and claps and I let out a few whistles, which causes a couple of girls from my class to turn around and giggle. (Those girls are always giggling, and I find this both strange and annoying.)

Luke responds with a shrug. "Not my game," he mumbles on the way to pick up his trash.

After our lunches are finished (well, the good parts, at least), we pack up our stuff and head outside to enjoy our last bit of freedom before the bell rings for afternoon classes.

"So, a little one-on-one?" I ask Luke, gesturing to the basketball nets.

"You're hilarious," he replies, sarcastically.

"No, I think Jay is right. You should definitely show off some more of your moves. I mean . . . you've got skills," Max chimes in, grinning.

"Oh, you don't think I've got skills? Would a guy

without skills be able to do this?" Luke knocks off Max's hat with one hand and catches it with other. He tosses it my way, I catch it, and I throw it back as Max comes toward me.

We spend the rest of the lunch hour playing keep-away with Max's hat, which I realize is kind of an immature game but . . . what can I say? It's hilarious. And I never claimed to be mature.

✖ ✖ ✖

My mom says that I am a "procrastinator," which I thought sounded really cool the first time I heard it. Doesn't it totally sound like an awesome movie with a lot of fighting and aliens and robots and no kissing? Wouldn't you go see a movie called The Procrastinator? Unfortunately, being a procrastinator actually means leaving everything to the last minute. And when I learned that, well, it just didn't seem like it would be much of movie if it was just some guy sitting around NOT doing anything. (Although you could still have a cool movie tagline like, "The Procrastinator: This deadline might be deadly," or something like that. Okay, you might have to tweak it a little, but what do I look like, a screenwriter?) At any rate, I am a procrastinator. This is probably why I have waited until November before approaching Mrs. Jennings about a music tutor.

I guess I kind of thought that if I continued to pretend to play along with the rest of my section it might eventually translate into . . . uh . . . actually playing? I know, the theory wasn't without flaws, but I heard someone once say that you have to "fake it until you make it." Apparently, that person has never fake-played a saxophone.

It's just after Music class and I take my time putting away my gear (or whatever music people call their . . . stuff) before making my way up to Mrs. Jennings's desk. At least, I assume it's a desk. The top is covered with papers and mugs and small plaques that say things like, "You'd better C Sharp or you're going to B Flat." Here are a few more:

- "Life should be a crescendo!"
- "Treble maker"
- "If it's not Baroque, don't fix it!"

I have no idea what any of these mean.

Mrs. Jennings is sitting behind the giant mess, humming so furiously to herself that she does not even notice me standing there.

"Excuse me . . . Mrs. Jennings?"

"Oh! My dear . . . I didn't see you! When the music takes over, well . . . you know!"

I don't know.

"Sure . . . well, I was kind of hoping that I could talk to you about—"

"About the saxophone. Of course, dear. I've noticed that you've been struggling a bit in class, but you know what they say, practice makes perfect!"

"Right. Practice. You see, that's kind of what I was hoping to talk—"

"I remember when I was just a young musical artist like yourself. The first time I sat down at a piano, my fingers touching the glossy black and white keys, the sound of the metronome . . . tick, tick, tick, tick . . ."

Mrs. Jennings has that far-off look in her eyes, and I know I need to pull her down to earth before I lose her for good.

"I want a tutor!"

Mrs. Jennings immediately snaps back into reality and gives me a puzzled look. I'm not quite sure if she's confused because I want a tutor, or just . . . confused.

"I mean . . . I was hoping I could get a tutor, if that's possible . . . please."

"I'm sure we could arrange that. But you know, I always say that the *soul*," she clutches her chest and gives a dramatic pause, "is the best tutor." She stares at me.

I stare back. Am I supposed to say something? Is there a proper amount of time to make it seem like that's really "sunk in"?

"I have the perfect tutor for you. I'll get back to you with a date and time," Mrs. Jennings says hurriedly, and then she immediately returns to her humming.

I leave the classroom only 75 percent sure that my tutor will be an actual human being.

✖ ✖ ✖

After only a few more classes, school is over for the day and I get to go over to Luke's house. We don't have practice today and as much as I love hockey, I'm kind of stoked to be able to just chill out for a couple of hours.

We immediately go to the kitchen to get a snack. Luke's mom is what one might refer to as a "health nut," so there's always a bowl on the counter with nutritious snacks. Most of the time the stuff is pretty good, although there always seems to be an alarming amount of seeds in everything she bakes. This not only makes the texture of her peanut butter cookies a little strange but has also led to embarrassing scenarios in which I have been alerted to the fact that there are tiny black seeds between my teeth. Needless to say, I have started to do a once-over in the mirror before leaving Luke's place. Today, the bowl is full of a bunch of fruit, and the baking looks fairly safe. We grab a couple of things and then head out to the driveway to shoot some pucks off of Luke's garage door.

As soon as we step outside, my ears are instantly frozen. I put on a toque and pull some gloves out of my coat pockets. Parry Sound winters are for REAL. You pretty much have to have a hat and a pair of gloves on you at all times, and a spare set not far away. This one time, a bunch of us were going to play pond hockey and I couldn't find any of my pairs of gloves. Dylan was wearing his and had left his other set at school, so my only option was a pair of Jodie's. They were purple with sparkly silver thread sewn into the fabric, and they looked absolutely ridiculous on me. But I wore them. Like I said, Parry Sound winters are for REAL.

"So," Luke is dumping a bunch of pucks out of a netted bag, "what were you doing after Music class, anyway? I was trying to find you to show you some new cheat codes for our game before Social Studies."

"I was . . . I decided to ask her about a tutor," I say, taking my first shot. "I guess she's gonna hook me up with someone."

"So, you haven't figured it out yet? I mean, how hard can it be to play the saxophone?" Luke takes a shot and it hits just to the right of the X that we have stuck to the garage door with duct tape.

"Says the guy whose instrument is basically a big bucket you hit with sticks." I take my next shot, but at the last moment the stick slips and the puck goes whirling too much to the left.

Luke grins. "Can I help it my last name starts with a B? You should really file for a legal name change." He shoots again, still just a little to the right.

"Tell me about it. But I doubt that I can manage that before our Music test. So . . . tutor it is."

"Well, good luck with that," Luke says, still grinning.

"Hey, keep laughing," I say, pulling back my stick. I focus on the garage door target and bring the stick down, sending the puck flying forward to hit the mark directly in the center of the X.

Luke whistles. "Well, you've got that going for ya."

We continue taking turns shooting pucks against the door, not noticing that it's getting dark, until Luke's dad calls him in.

"What time is it, Dad?" Luke shouts back.

"It's 5:15," his dad says, walking out to put some garbage by the curb.

"I gotta go or I'm gonna be late for dinner," I say, putting away the sticks and dropping the pucks into the bag before I start walking home.

"Hey, the Bruins are playing the Habs tonight, right?" Luke says, shoving the bin to the side of the driveway.

How could I have forgotten?

"Yeah," I call over my shoulder, already starting my walk home. "See ya!"

I barely manage to get to the table before dinner is served. We eat our dinner (something gray and mushy), and as soon as the meal is over I race up the stairs to my bedroom to quickly do my homework before the game starts. As soon as the last math problem is completed, I grab my jersey (aka, one of the few things I would grab in a fire) and toss it on. It is, of course, a Boston Bruins jersey. And you can probably guess what's on the back:

ORR

4

In the living room my whole family has taken their usual positions: Mom and Dad are on the loveseat, Jodie is sitting cross-legged on the floor, and Dylan is spread out on the couch. I take my place in an armchair, and Dylan tosses me a half-empty bag of licorice. On the coffee table in front of him is a wide variety of chips and candy, along with a couple of cans of pop. Everyone is wearing their jerseys, silently waiting for the face-off. The only sounds in the room are the crunching and chewing and sipping and slurping.

This is what a Boston Bruins game night looks like in my house. It is the one activity that no one misses, the one family night no one complains about. From the day you are born a Roberts you are taught the sacred tradition of being a Boston Bruins fan (and, by extension, a Bobby Orr fan, because one simply cannot exist without the other). Game nights just become a part of who you are and what you do. And there is no better game night on the planet than the lineup tonight:

Boston Bruins

vs.

Montreal Canadiens

Boston and Montreal (or the Habs, as they are traditionally called) are longtime rivals, so you KNOW it is going to be a good game. Tonight we have the home-ice advantage, but that doesn't mean much when you have two teams who are ready to play with a vengeance.

"Hey, can you pass the licorice, Jay?" Jodie asks, her hand sticking out toward me. Usually, she would say something like, "Hey, you gonna eat the whole bag or you gonna give me some?" or something to that effect, but there is kind of an unwritten sibling truce on game night.

"Sure. Here," I say, tossing the bag.

"Boston Garden. Man, I'd love to see a game there again," my dad says. "I was just six years old when your

Grandpa Joe took me to see a game at the Garden. It was 1974, before Bobby Orr retired. And your old man got to see him in action. I've told you about that game, right?"

He has. A million times. But we sit and listen to it again because he tells it with such excitement that it's almost like being there watching it with him. I've seen footage of Bobby Orr, but I can't imagine what it would be like to see him play in an actual arena. Listening to my Grandpa Joe and my dad talk about it is just about the closest I'll ever get to the real thing.

As soon as the puck is dropped the silence returns until the game really gets going. Then the room is filled with a lot of shouting and frustrated grunts and cheering. I have to admit that on nights like this, my family almost seems . . . not half bad.

✖ ✖ ✖

Nothing much happens over the next week, and on Thursday morning I wake up the way I normally do— to the sound of Jodie's hair dryer and Dylan's music blasting from their respective rooms. A yawn escapes my mouth, and as I sleepily push the warm blanket to the side I start thinking about what I need to do to prepare for the day's events. (Side note: Luke has often made fun of me at sleepovers because he feels that I need to replace my bed covers with something more "age-appropriate." True, my blanket may or may not have bears on it. And they may or may not be dancing. And they may or may not be wearing brightly colored T-shirts with alphabet letters on them. But in my defense, it is the softest, most comfortable blanket ever made. And sometimes, a good blanket just has to come before style. I have no regrets.)

Okay, what do I have going on today? . . . Math in the morning, so I'll need to stick my homework in my binder. Social Studies in the afternoon, and I'm just about out of lined paper in that binder so I'll need to refill it. History textbook, lunch bag . . . wait. Lunch. Something is happening at lunch. What am I doing at . . . ? RIGHT. Today is the day I'm meeting with my new tutor at lunchtime. Just thinking about it makes me groan. Don't get me wrong—I am happy to be getting the help, and I'll be even happier if this means I have a chance at passing my Music test, but giving up my lunch hour for the saxophone? Yeah, not exactly my idea of a fun time.

Plus, I have no idea what to expect. I mean, I've had plenty of coaches—is a tutor kind of like that? It's possible, although I'm fairly certain he/she will not be running anything that resembles a flow drill in hockey (a drill where you literally don't stop until the coach blows the whistle . . . it's pretty killer).

GAME TIP #8: *You would think this would go without saying, but never participate in a burrito-eating contest before practice when you know the coach will be running a flow drill. I mean, c'mon . . . that's just common sense.*

The morning goes by without incident and I have all but forgotten about my lunch meeting until I run into Luke at his locker.

"Let's go, I'm starving," I say to Luke as he grabs his lunch, shoves his backpack into his locker, and shuts the door.

"Um, I thought you had something over lunch hour . . . your saxophone thing, right?"

I let out my second groan of the day. "Oh man . . . I gotta head over there right now or I'll totally be late."

"Enjoy yourself . . . and try not to think of me eating my lunch, you know . . . relaxing, nothing to worry about . . ."

"Yeah, yeah. Catch ya later."

I go back to my locker to grab my saxophone and glance at the large clock in the hallway. It's almost noon. I shove my sandwich into my mouth on my way to the music room, accidentally dropping some crumbs and a few pieces of lettuce behind me. I would normally take the time to clean up after myself but I really do not want to be late for my first tutoring session. Besides, if

I pass out while attempting to play the saxophone, at least Luke will have a trail to follow to find me.

I enter the room and spy Mrs. Jennings, who is talking wildly, complete with exaggerated hand gestures, to some kid who is attempting to eat a bag of chips.

"... and that is why we must pass the gift of music to all who seek it!" The boy does not look convinced but nods his head slightly. "Ah! There is he is now! Jason, I would like you to meet Benjamin Davidson." Benjamin is a tall, lanky kid with a face full of freckles and thick, dark-rimmed glasses. I think I've seen him around the school once or twice, and I'm pretty sure he is in seventh or eighth grade.

He grins at me and sticks out his hand. "Hi there, I'm Ben!" It seems weird that his hand is extended toward me since no kid has shaken another kid's hand since 1950 ... but I shake it all the same.

"Well, now that we have the introductions out of the way, I'll leave you to it!" With that, Mrs. Jennings leaps, literally LEAPS out of the classroom. I turn to see if Ben is laughing but he's already opening his saxophone case and putting the instrument together. Now, you should know, I'm a pretty shy guy. I'm not usually the one to begin conversations, but given this is a bit of an awkward situation, I feel as though I should try in some way to break the ice with this Ben kid.

"So, you got stuck with the saxophone too, eh? They seriously need to start making class lists that start from Z and work their way up." Ben looks up at me, seemingly confused. "You know, because all the kids with last names at the top of the list get to pick things first?"

"I didn't get stuck with the saxophone, I picked it! I'd already learned the trumpet and the flute, and I really wanted to give myself a bit of a challenge." He grins again and continues to put the pieces of his saxophone in place. Great. Just great. I've got one of "those" kids, the kind of kid who wants a "challenge." You know what kids who like challenges also like?

1. Learning random facts about lizards . . . because it's just so interesting!
2. Eating twelve-grain bread.
   (TWELVE grains? Is that really necessary?)
3. Raising their hand multiple times in class.
   (Give it a REST already.)
4. Being the teacher's pet . . . enough said.

Now, before you start saying, "Don't judge a book by its cover, Jay," let's just be honest. We all judge books by their covers. I mean, if you had picked up this book in the library or a bookstore and the cover had a picture of some kid giving a thumbs-up and the title read something like *How to Be Your Best You!* it's more than likely that you never would have opened it to page one. (Unless you want to learn how to be the best you . . . in which case, I don't know how to tell you this, but you are probably reading the wrong book.) So yes, I know that everyone says we are not supposed to judge someone that we don't know, but even if I don't KNOW this kid Ben, trust me . . . I know his type. I have met his type. I have sat next to his type. It's not that I have a problem with kids like Ben . . . it's just that I can't understand them. AT ALL.

"It's going to be pretty hard to play that, you know." Ben is looking intently at me and I realize I have probably been out of it for a few minutes. Mrs. Jennings must be rubbing off on me.

"I . . . I know, that's why I thought I should get a tutor."

Ben laughs, a nerdy, high-pitched laugh, and opens my case. "No, I mean it's going to be pretty hard to play that if it's in the case."

"Oh. Right." I start taking out my saxophone and glance at the clock: 12:15. Maybe Ben can teach me how to play the saxophone in forty-five minutes and I'll be done with tutoring and him forever.

"Now, I should warn you, you're not going to learn the saxophone in a day. It's going to take time, a lot of hard work, and a ton of practice. I'm thinking we should set up a tutoring schedule . . . maybe twice a week, Tuesdays and Thursdays?"

Waste another fifty or so lunch hours? Yep, that sounds about right. Let's check the score:

JAY   SAXOPHONE

0 2

CHAPTER 6

"Ready?" Ben is sitting across from me with his saxophone strapped around his neck.

"I guess," I reply, which in this case means NOT AT ALL AND I WILL NEVER GET THIS SO WE MIGHT AS WELL STOP TRYING. By the way, Ben is giving me that goofy grin again, so I can tell he doesn't get the hidden meaning.

"Okay, the first thing you're going to do is put your instrument together."

After two months of Music classes, it's the only thing I can actually do. Without faking it.

"Okay, good. Now, attach the reed and tighten the ligature."

Ligature. Apparently the weird metal thing has a name! I am absolutely thrilled by this new knowledge. Can you tell?

"Great. Now attach the strap, put it around your neck, and show me how you hold your instrument."

I follow his instructions, holding the saxophone the way I do in class. Wait, I lied before. That's TWO things. I can do TWO things with my saxophone.

"That's good, just loosen your grip a little bit with your left hand, and your right hand should be farther down."

"That feels weird," I complain, trying to reposition my right hand to feel more comfortable.

"Trust me, by the time we're finished, it will feel as normal as breathing." Yeah, um . . . not likely, Ben. "Okay, so now that we've got a better hand position, we'll use the rest of our session to work on our embouchure."

"Omba-what?"

"Embouchure. It's how your mouth is positioned in order to make a good sound with your instrument. It's one of the most important things you need to know in order to play the saxophone, so we have to make sure we've got it down before we start playing."

"So, we're going to spend the rest of our lunch hour . . . NOT playing the saxophone?" At this pace, no wonder he wants to meet twice a week. This guy really needs to work on his time management.

"Look, you need to be able to do this in order to make a decent sound. Playing the saxophone is more than just holding down a key and blowing into your mouthpiece. You have to have the right foundation in order to ensure your tone production is right. There are so many elements to making music, which is one of the reasons it's so satisfying when you finally master it. For instance . . ."

He keeps talking, but I'm not really listening. I just need to be able to play a few notes on a saxophone, and Ben seems a little too intense for my purposes. I wonder if it's possible to make a tutor switch, or switch my instrument, or switch my school . . .

"So, let's give it a try," Ben is saying, and I am starting to realize that I have a major focus problem.

"Uh . . . right. We're giving what a try, exactly?" I ask, hoping he doesn't realize that I have not been listening for the past five minutes.

"Your embouchure. Everyone's is a bit different but it kind of looks like this." Ben starts slightly pulling in his bottom lip and pushing out his top lip. It is all I can do not to laugh out loud, until he motions for me to try. I look around to make sure no one is in the vicinity, and start imitating Ben's lip pose.

"Okay, that's a good start. Try to put your top lip out just a bit more. That's better, relax your lips . . ."

"Awww, taking a few kissing lessons, Squirt?" I turn around and there's Mick Bartlet, arms crossed, leaning in the door frame. Of course it *had* to be Mick. Immediately, my lips stop doing the *omba*-thingy and I attempt to act natural, which of course makes me look totally unnatural.

Ben starts saying, "Sorry, this is a closed tutoring session. If you need help, you can schedule with Mrs.—" Mick cuts him off.

"Yeah, I think I can figure out how to blow into a horn, but thanks."

"There's a lot more involved in perfecting your musical craft than simply producing a sound out of an instrument. For instance, one must consider proper pitch and tone," Ben says, starting to give Mick the same lecture he gave me. This time, I'm the one that cuts him off.

"What do you want, Mick?" I ask, although I'm sure I already know the answer.

"Oh, I was just passing by and thought you might like an audience. You're a regular musical genius, Roberts. Standing ovation! Bravo! Encore!" Mick begins to applaud and whistle. When the bell rings he pretends to tip an imaginary hat my way and leaves the music room, laughing. I quickly start taking my saxophone apart, never more grateful that lunch hour is over.

"So, keep practicing your embouchure, and I'll see you back here on Tuesday?"

"Yep, sure thing." I hastily stick the pieces of my saxophone into the case and get up to leave. Even though it was even worse than I'd imagined, I hear my mom's voice in my brain, reminding me to use my manners. I reach the door and turn around to face Ben, who is still putting his saxophone away.

"Uh, thanks," I say, awkwardly.

Ben smiles. "No, problem. See you later."

I nod and walk out of the room, thinking about how much I don't want "later" to come.

✕ ✕ ✕

I have hockey practice after school so I get home as quickly as possible to grab a light snack before I go. Practice goes smoothly, mostly because Mick is not there. He started feeling sick near the end of the school day and one of his friends told the coach he went home with the flu, which is pretty incredible considering the kid is almost never sick. He has, like, some super immunity to sickness or something. (Side note: Just in case you didn't know, having an "immunity" means that you have built up a resistance to something. For example, I am currently trying to become immune to my mom's tuna casserole. I force myself to take one extra bite every time I eat it and to keep it down. So far, I'm up to eight.)

To my amazement, when I get home after practice, the TV is Jodie-and-Dylan-free. Jodie is in her
room and Dylan is at a friend's house. This means I
have full access to the TV, without having to fight either
of my siblings about what we're going to watch, for
a full fifteen minutes until dinner's ready. After a few
moments of looking for the remote (which is under
a hoodie Jodie left draped over one of the chairs) I
settle into the couch and hit power. I haven't even had
a moment to look through the channels when I hear
my mom calling.

"Jason? Jason, honey!"

"Yeah, mom?" I hit the mute button.

"Do you have homework to do?"

"Mom, I just got home."

"Interesting, that doesn't sound like an answer to
my question."

"I have a tiny bit of Social Studies. I'll finish it after
dinner."

My mom has now entered the living room. "What
about Music? I haven't heard any saxophone sounds
coming from your bedroom." Apparently, I can't escape
the saxophone even long enough to watch a TV show.

"I . . . I'm working on my . . . *omba* . . . *shurm* right
now, you know, really getting the foundation laid for
playing my instrument," I say, stealing a line from Ben.

"Really? Well, I'm glad to hear you're taking the sax-ophone so seriously. I know that music's not really your thing, and I thought you might be a little bit nervous about having to play an instrument in front of people." My mom sits down beside me on the couch, and I can tell she is ready to have one of *those* conversations. My mom has an amazing ability to know exactly what I am upset about before I even tell her I'm upset about it. It's like a weird, mom X-ray thing she has going on.

"Yeah, well . . . I mean, I'm not super excited about it or anything. But I'm getting someone to tutor me at school, so I'm sure I'll get the hang of it."

"Well, I'm proud of you for being so responsible and getting a tutor. And I know you can do whatever you put your mind to," my mom says, patting me on the back. That's every parent's line when they know you're going to be bad at something.

"Thanks, Mom," I say, hoping our conversation might be over.

"You know, I can kind of relate to what you're going through," she continues, and my hope immediately vanishes. "When I was young, I had to give a speech in front of the whole class, and there was nothing I hated more than talking in front of people. I stressed out about it for months, and I could barely sleep the whole week before."

"Let me guess . . . you practiced really hard and the speech went fine and everything worked out," I finished for her.

"Oh, not at all. I forgot an entire section in the middle, left the room crying, and threw up in the bathroom."

"Um . . . thanks, Mom, that . . . that really helps."

My mom laughs a little and moves closer to me on the couch. "My point is, I'm still sitting here today . . . I got through it! Everyone has their own talents, and not everyone is good at everything. Someone who is really good at music might not have the skills you have to play hockey. All your father and I expect of you is to do your best, your very best, at whatever you do," my mom pauses, "and try not to throw up," she adds, nudging me.

"I'll see what I can do," I say as my mom gives me a squeeze and gets up from the couch. Finally able to relax and watch a show, I un-mute the TV just as the front door opens.

"I am not watching one of your dumb cartoons," I hear Jodie say behind me.

Awesome.

✖ ✖ ✖

I wake up on Saturday with just one thought:
It's Game Day.

Sometimes it feels like the only reason for getting through the week is to make it to Saturday, as if it is the only "real" day. I don't allow myself to worry about school or the saxophone, and even though I will have to see Mick in a few hours (apparently it was only a twenty-four-hour flu . . . just my luck), I don't let myself think about him, either. Today it's all about the game. I go through my routine, which includes eating a good breakfast, making sure all of my gear is packed, and yelling outside the bathroom door for Jodie to get out so that I can get in. Even through the door I can *hear* her eye-rolls.

Luke's parents are driving us to the rink this particular Saturday and I barely make it to his house on time since I had to wait FOREVER to get into the bathroom. When I arrive, Luke is having a conversation with his mom that I've overhead a million times before.

"Mom, it's gross!"

"You need energy, Lukey. This smoothie has spinach, quinoa, eggs, and six different kinds of nutritional powders." Luke's mom is handing him a glass of terrible-looking green mush.

"Which is exactly why it's GROSS," Luke says, attempting to hand it back. He sees me and hollers in my direction, "Back me up, Jay!"

"It looks absolutely delicious and nutritious, Mrs. Benson," I say with a smile.

Luke scowls and tries to hand the glass to me. "Then YOU drink it."

"Oh, I am already too full from the healthy breakfast my own mother was sweet enough to prepare for me," I respond, smiling once more at Luke's mom.

Luke shakes his head, plugs his nose, and guzzles more than half of the green stuff. He makes a gagging sound, gulps down the last bit, and puts the glass down on the table.

"There. Gotta go."

"What about the flaxseed biscuits I made?" Mrs. Benson is saying as we make our play for the front door.

"Really appreciate the support back there, Ralph," Luke grumbles sarcastically.

"Listen, Lukey . . . you need energy to play, and the better you play, the better the game goes. I'm just thinking of the team, here."

Luke slaps my stick so that it falls out of my hand to the ground, laughs, and sprints ahead. I pick up my stick, jog a little to catch up with him, and start loading my equipment into his parents' car.

"You see? Look at all the energy that glass of goodness has given you!"

Luke mumbles some kind of sarcastic comeback as he gets into the backseat, but by the time we get to the rink he seems to have forgotten all about it. We quickly get changed, and in a few minutes Luke and I are skating around our half of the ice while a few of our teammates take some shots on goal to warm up. As I stride forward I can hear the sound of hockey sticks making contact with pucks.

Slap. Slap. Slap.

Now THAT'S a rhythm I can appreciate. It does almost sound musical, although I'm pretty sure that's just my overactive brain, not quite shut off from my tutoring session. I shake off all thoughts of music and concentrate on the task at hand. It's time to focus.

It's hockey time.

I can't remember when I first became interested in the game. It's as if it was always just part of me. You know—arms, legs, hockey. I have often thought how awesome it would be if, instead of arms, I had two hockey sticks. I could probably even be some kind of superhero. You know, a hockey team is down by five points and it seems as though all is lost. But all of a sudden, "It's Captain Hockey!" I whizz around their opponents because my skates have been outfitted with rockets—obviously—and I score a whole bunch of goals in the last three minutes to win the game. Then again, making a peanut butter sandwich would be a little bit of an issue.

Wait. Where was I again? Right. Hockey. It's not that I don't like other sports. Baseball is all right. I like soccer. And I'm actually pretty good at golf. But being on the ice just feels so natural, like my body instinctively knows what to do, almost as if my skates are somehow in control of me . . .

BAM.

All right, maybe I don't have as much control as I thought.

GAME TIP #9: *When skating, it is in your best interest to concentrate on what you're doing and not start thinking about other stuff. Because you are on ICE. With a pair of thin BLADES strapped to your feet. So, yeah. FOCUS.*

I feel myself falling and I hit the ice with a thud. For a moment I am confused. How did I end up on my back?

And then I hear Mick Bartlet.

"Hey, Jay! Drop something?"

Mick is skating away, laughing with a couple of his friends, and I can see Luke skating back toward me. I've had just about enough of Mick and his annoying antics, and as I get myself up from the ice, I think about skating over and giving him a piece of my mind. But I know that guys like Mick thrive on getting guys like me riled up and I won't give him the satisfaction. Luke is beside me now, and before he can open his mouth the referee blows his whistle, signaling that the game is about to begin. As I skate toward the center circle for the opening face-off I can still hear Mick chuckling, but it doesn't matter. The game is about to begin, and I'm in the starting lineup.

The puck is dropped.

Game on.

This is not the first time we've played the Wolves this season. They're a pretty good team, but we can hold our own, and the first period is mostly uneventful. A lot of shots from both teams but nothing sticks. I am able to head up ice a few times and get some shots on target, but their defense is pretty tight, and more times than not the puck is gone before I even get a good chance.

The second period is a little more exciting, and halfway through we score a goal with twenty seconds left on a power play. But the other team keeps pace, scoring two minutes later to tie it up.

It's not until the third period that things really start to get intense.

We stay tied for most of the period, but around eighteen minutes in, our goaltender makes a sweet glove save. He drops the puck to his stick and quickly shovels it toward our right-winger, Kyle. Kyle starts to skate and attempts a pass to Ryan, on the left, but no luck. It's intercepted, and as soon as I see that the other team has possession I get ready for their attack. They drive toward our net and take a shot, which I'm able to get down and block at the last minute. I go after the puck and for a moment it's mine, but someone makes a stellar move that lifts my stick and suddenly they have it again. Another shot. I hear the puck smack off the goal post and then see Mick and an opponent heading toward the puck along the side boards. Mick reaches in to grab the puck and BAM! He's down.

And then it happens.

Before getting run over, Mick manages to tap the puck up to Luke, who starts to head toward the other end of the ice. I glance up at the clock: eighteen seconds left in the game.

Lots of time.

I start to follow Luke up ice, and when he gets sealed off at the center line, I suddenly find a loose puck coming right to me. I keep my feet moving, pull a little move around one of their players, and break into an opening. I can hear my teammates start to count down the remaining seconds from the bench.

Ten ... nine ...

We always do that to let everyone on the ice know exactly how much time is left in a period. Only now, it's how much time is left in the game. I cross their blue line and look for a shot, but the angle isn't very good, and there's a big defenseman between me and the net.

Eight ... seven ...

I decide to gamble, go around their player, hold the puck and head toward the back of the net. I want to try the wraparound, but their goalie is onto me and slides across the crease, leaving me nothing to shoot at as I circle around the other side.

Six ... five ... four ... three ...

Out of time. I might as well try to put something in the net. I'm ready to shoot, pulling my stick back, when out of the corner of my eye I see him. Mick Bartlet has managed to join the attack and is standing unattended on the other side of the net. His stick is on the ice, a big target. I send him a quick, sharp pass, he redirects it, and just like that, the puck is in the net.

It's like in the movies. The buzzer sounds just after the puck crosses the goal line. We've won the game. Everyone crowds around Mick, the victor, the hero. Final score: 2–1.

It's a bit annoying, watching everyone gush over Mick's winning goal, especially when I set it up for him and I know there was a chance that I could have scored if I'd taken the shot myself. (I'll get my point for the assist, but let's be honest, people who actually put the puck in the net get most of the attention.) But as my coach always says, part of being a good player is knowing when to shoot the puck and when to pass it. Mick had a better shot, it was as simple as that. And at the end of the game, whatever the player stats—I only care about the two numbers on the scoreboard. And let's be honest—I prefer my team to have the higher one.

I'll even take a goal from Mick Bartlet to get it.

CHAPTER 7

By December, the Shamrocks are 9 and 3, which means we have won 9 games and lost 3. Not bad, right? The last few weeks of school have been going okay, with the exception of the saxophone, which has definitely not been going okay, even though I have been attending my tutoring classes every week and kind of practicing. But that's not really on my mind right now. There is only one thing a kid thinks about in the month of December: Christmas Break.

The first week of December is always the worst because Christmas Break is just close enough that you can almost taste the freedom and yet far enough away that it makes every day seem to drag on forever. During this time, teachers lose their minds and start piling on assignments and research projects at an alarming rate. So you're going about your business, just trying to keep it together for a few more weeks, and then, out of nowhere . . . complete and utter schoolwork chaos.

Example: As if I don't have enough stress in my life, my science teacher thought he would make things just a LITTLE more terrible by giving us a GROUP ASSIGNMENT.

Group. Assignments. Are. The. Worst.

It doesn't make sense, but for some reason, no matter how many kids are in the class, there never seems to be the right number for the groups to split up evenly. So when you finally find a few people you like well enough to do a project with, and feel somewhat confident that by the end you will not want to duct tape them to a wall, you end up getting an extra person added to the mix that totally throws off the balance.

For instance, take this science group assignment. Luke, Max, and I are the perfect mix of intelligence and fun. Sure, part of our "research" will include playing video games and eating chips, but when it comes down to it, the three of us will make sure it gets done. Add one person, just ONE more person, and the whole thing falls apart. Which is exactly what is about to happen.

"Kaylee? You haven't found a group yet? Let's see . . . why don't I add you to Jay's photosynthesis group?" my science teacher says, and he directs her over to my table.

Kaylee Gifford. Perfect. Kaylee is one of those "I know everything" types who enjoy making everyone else feel like they know nothing. (If you don't believe me, please refer to the saxophone-reed-monkey-on-my-shoulder incident of Chapter Three.) She will completely take over every aspect of this project, including, but not limited to: the thickness of the report cover, the type of font for the report, the pictures on the display board, the lettering on the display board, the color of the display board, and she will even dictate when we will . . .

"So, we can meet at my place today at 4:30. Here's my address for you to copy into your agendas. Don't ring the doorbell because my mother has sensitive ears," Kaylee says, shoving a piece of paper into the middle of the table.

. . . meet. Well, that's fantastic. Not only do I hate group projects to begin with, but now this project has been completely hijacked. *This day could not get any worse*, I think as I start copying down Kaylee's perfectly printed address into my notebook. Just then, the bell rings for lunch hour and I almost have to laugh.

Can't get any worse? Right. Except for the fact that now I have to go play the saxophone.

✗ ✗ ✗

I walk into the music room to find Ben sitting in a chair, playing a few notes on his instrument and tapping his toes as he plays. When he sees me he stops momentarily, gives me a slight wave, and then continues where he left off.

By now, I know the drill of putting my instrument together, which, if nothing else, I can do pretty easily. Ben is still playing, but when he notices I have my saxophone together he finishes the tune and turns to face me.

"Okay, so now make sure you're holding your instrument properly." Even though we've been doing this for a couple of weeks, and I should definitely have it down by now, I still fumble my hands around for a few seconds, and it never seems to look quite right.

"It looks way better than when you first started," Ben says, repositioning my hands just a bit. "Okay, let's take a look at your embouchure. You're still practicing it at home, right?"

I nod.

I have not once, at any time, practiced my embouchure.

I stick out my lips and make a kind of fish face, hoping that all weird-looking lip poses kind of fit into the embouchure category.

"No . . . the top lip kind of goes over the bottom lip, and the lips are relaxed, not tight, remember?" Ben is showing me with his own mouth and I am only half-trying to imitate him, partly because I think there is no way this will actually help me play the saxophone and partly because I'm nervous that Mick will show up again. At any rate, one might say my heart isn't really in it.

"C'mon, Jay. You've got to learn to do this. I know it

feels funny, but like I said before, you'll get used to it."

I am now feeling a tiny bit annoyed and I stop doing the lip thing completely. "Even if I do learn this *omba-shurm* thing . . ."

"Embouchure," Ben corrects.

"Whatever it is! Look, I haven't been able to play even a few notes together without making a giant squeak, and to say I have no sense of rhythm is the understatement of the century. If I can't do even this tiny thing, maybe I shouldn't waste my time trying to learn to play the saxophone. Why bother, when I know I am not going to be able to do it?"

"Well, with that attitude, of course you're never going to learn it. And I can tell that you haven't been practicing at all. It takes hard work and dedication to—"

"Seriously, are you, like, a teacher in disguise or something? What kid talks like that?"

Ben frowns and slumps down slightly in his chair, and I can tell I have hurt his feelings. I know I should apologize, that I should tell him that I'm just mad about being terrible at the saxophone, but instead I mumble some excuse about not feeling well and leave my tutoring session early.

That could have gone better.

✖ ✖ ✖

My afternoon classes seem slower than usual, and whenever I picture Ben's expression it makes a knot in my stomach. Ben's an okay guy. He was just trying to help me, and I was totally rude. I try to find him in the hallway after school, but I don't see him anywhere so I resolve to apologize the next day.

Luke comes to my house after school so that we can hang for an hour until it's time to go to Kaylee's. His eyes light up when he enters the kitchen and spots a huge mound of cookies that my dad brought home yesterday from the bakery next door to his shop. Luke stuffs one in his mouth, grabbing another two directly after.

"I seriously love coming to your house," Luke says, still chewing his cookie and showing me the entire contents of his mouth.

"Gross, dude. Didn't your parents ever teach you not to talk with your mouth full?"

Luke puts another cookie in his mouth, chews for a moment, and then opens it even wider. "What do you mean, Jay? Are you saying I don't have good manners?" Luke laughs, and I give him a sort of shove and grab a cookie for myself.

We play a video game until it's time to go (after all, it will no longer be a part of our "research") and then my mom drops us off at Kaylee's house.

"You two have fun, now!"

Yeah, Mom. This is going to be a real blast.

I pretty much nailed how this group project is going to go. Kaylee already has everything picked out and drones on about how presenting our work clearly and neatly is just as important as having good content. As she takes out a bunch of duotangs in different colors, Luke closes his eyes and makes a snoring noise, which catches Kaylee's attention.

"Luke!" Kaylee yells, giving him a stern look. Luke suddenly snaps to attention as if Kaylee's voice has woken him from a deep sleep.

"What? Huh? What day is this? Where am I?" Luke asks groggily.

"Oh, that is just so mature, Luke," Kaylee responds, with an eye-roll that could compete with Jodie's. Luke grins and looks for a high-five from me or Max, but Kaylee shoots us both a don't-you-dare look.

"Okay, so I've already found a bunch of research material. Luke, can I trust you to go downstairs to get it from the printer, or is that job too hard for your tiny, half-functional brain?"

"I'm not sure I can handle it, but maybe with the help of a friend . . ."

"I'll do it!" Max shouts, obviously trying to get out of whatever job Kaylee might assign him. Before she can respond, the two of them jump up and dash out of the room, leaving Kaylee and me alone. Thanks, guys.

"Great, it's already 5:30 and we've barely done anything. We should plan to meet at lunch tomorrow and Thursday."

"Okay, but I can't on Thursday. I've got . . . something to do," I say, a little embarrassed to explain.

"You and Luke reading stupid comics does not count as doing something," Kaylee replies, sorting through the stack of duotangs.

"It's not that . . . I have to . . . I have a saxophone tutor during lunch, okay?" I respond, feeling defensive for some reason.

"Oh. Well, hopefully you've figured out where to put the reed by now," Kaylee teases. Kaylee doesn't tease very well. The only way anyone would know she was teasing instead of just being mean is because her eyebrows go up, ever so slightly.

"Yeah, that's pretty much the only thing I've figured out at this point. I haven't even played a single note on the thing yet. I'm still trying to figure out the, you know, the lip thing." I have butchered the word too many times so I decide to not even try.

"Embouchure? Oh, that's, like, totally easy."

"Well, maybe for someone like you, but for someone like me, it's just another reason I'm going to fail my Music test."

"Fail it? Dramatic much? Here, I'll show you. You just make your lips look like grandpa lips." I laugh, but

Kaylee's glaring at me. "I'm serious. Pretend to talk like a grandpa, it works every time."

"I . . . I have no idea what you're talking about."

"Oh, come on. *Jash pu ya mow wike wis*," Kaylee commands, making what I can only assume are her "grandpa lips." I don't see any sign of the other guys coming back so I give it a shot.

"*Wike wis?*" I ask, trying to model my mouth after Kaylee's.

"*Goo . . . wewax ya mowf . . .*"

"*Ahwite . . . betta?*"

"*Mush betta!*"

Suddenly in walk Luke and Max with stacks of paper in hand.

I instinctively jump away from Kaylee and try to make it look as though I'm just casually licking my lips or something, which is ridiculous. They both burst out laughing, and when they finally gain control of themselves, Luke shakes his head and says, "I am not even going to ask."

"Yeah, well you wouldn't understand it if you did, so it's probably better that way," Kaylee responds. Her stern look has returned and I can tell that our little "moment" is over.

The rest of our time is spent figuring out which information we're going to use and who will be responsible for what. As demanding as Kaylee is, I have to admit that she does a pretty good job organizing a project.

Also, I feel like I'm finally learning how to correctly do embouchure.

Also, I learned how to say the word "embouchure."

Things might actually be starting to turn around for Jay Roberts!

"Jay can't do Thursday at lunch, so let's plan to meet again on Friday to work on our project, since we have the day off from school."

Do a school project? ON A DAY OFF FROM SCHOOL???

Things might actually be getting worse for Jay Roberts.

CHAPTER 8

I try to find Ben at school on Wednesday, but I don't see him, and I have to leave right after school for hockey practice. So, my Thursday tutoring session will be the first time I see him since the awkwardness that was our last session.

I take a deep breath and walk into the music room, ready to offer my lengthy, prepared apology, but Ben is nowhere to be seen. The room is empty. My heart beats faster. He's not coming. He quit. I have forever ruined my chances of not completely embarrassing myself because I refused to practice my embouchure and then freaked out on Ben. I mean, I totally deserve it. With my attitude, I would have quit on me too. But I thought, maybe if I apologized, maybe if I showed Ben I was ready to work hard, he might just give me one more chance . . .

"Hey! Sorry I'm late. I had a dentist appointment this morning that ran late. I just got back a couple of minutes ago." Ben is quickly walking toward his chair, looking a little out of sorts.

I don't say anything for a moment, trying to absorb the fact that Ben hasn't quit on me after all. "Oh . . . that . . . that's great . . . I mean, that you're here. I thought maybe . . . you'd decided not to tutor me any more," I stammer.

"Huh? What would make you think that?" Ben looks genuinely confused.

"Well, it's just . . . last time, I got really frustrated and I said that stuff to you and I'm super sorry . . . and then you weren't here . . ."

Ben lets out a small chuckle and smiles. "Look, I know this isn't easy for you. I expect that you will have moments of frustration, it's part of the learning process. But if you're still willing to learn the saxophone, I'm still willing to teach you. Assuming, of course, that you're ready to work."

"Definitely. I've even been practicing my embouchure. For real this time! Check this out." I do my best grandpa face, trying to remember to keep my mouth relaxed.

"Hey, good job! Not bad at all!"

I give a kind of half-smile. This is definitely the first time someone has given me praise for making a silly face. But, as strange as it sounds, getting this one thing right feels almost as good as it does when I make a great play on the ice. No. I take that back. It doesn't feel like that at all. But it also doesn't feel terrible to be able do something I couldn't before.

"Okay, now that you've just about got that down, you ready to move on?" I nod, and Ben continues. "So, let's see you hold the instrument again."

I put the strap around my neck and hold the saxophone the way Ben taught me.

"All right, we're getting there. I can tell you're really concentrating on where the hands need to go, but you need to start getting a feel for it. It's kind of like . . . like, holding a hockey stick. You play, right?"

Surprised, I stare at Ben for a minute. "Yeah, I play." Why is Ben "I like a challenge" talking about hockey?

"All right, so when you pick up a stick, do you have to remember where each hand goes?" Ben asks.

I laugh. "No, I just . . . know how to do it."

"But you didn't always know. Someone showed you how to hold it, and at some point, it became natural. And now, I bet you can't imagine how it felt before you could hold a stick. Do you shoot right or left?" Ben is taking off his saxophone and standing up.

"I shoot left. Wait . . . what does this have to do with—?"

"Just follow me for a second. Let's say you're getting ready to take a shot. Where are your hands?"

"Um, my right hand would be at the top of the stick and the—"

"No, show me."

This tutoring class is going in a strange direction, but I would rather be doing anything other than awkwardly holding this saxophone, so I play along. I stand up and pretend to grip my hockey stick.

"Okay, let's say I put this hand up here instead. What would that do?"

"Make me look totally lame?"

Ben is rolling his eyes. "I mean, how would that affect, say, how you shoot a puck?"

"I guess, I don't know . . . without the right grip, I wouldn't be able to shoot the same."

"Exactly! Playing a musical instrument is just like that. You have to have the proper grip in order to play it right." Ben seems excited, and even I have to admit that this tutoring thing isn't so bad now that hockey is involved. That being said, these past couple of chapters have had an alarming amount of saxophone and not enough hockey. So, just to keep you interested, here's a random hockey picture:

"Okay, so having the right grip is the first step. But what else could affect your shot?"

"A lot of things. I mean, my stance, how I control the puck . . ."

"Good, good! So you have to have the proper grip on your stick to be able to shoot correctly, just like you have to hold your instrument the right way in order to play music. And in hockey, you have to have a proper stance, which is kind of like having the right embouchure in music."

That makes sense.

"So once you have the right grip," Ben adjusts my hands slightly, "and the right stance, the last thing you need to do is hit the note. In hockey, just before you let a shot go you have to pull back the stick, right? Well, to play the saxophone, pulling back the stick would be equivalent to breathing in air. You breathe in, then blow out on the mouthpiece. How you blow on the mouthpiece will determine how the note sounds, similar to how you connect with the puck. Get it?"

"Okaaay . . . so . . . what's the best way to do it?"

"Honestly, the best way is for you to just start trying it. I mean, your coaches give you tips about how to shoot better, but don't you find a lot of your improvement comes from just trying out stuff on the ice?"

I see his point. "So I should just . . . give it a go?"

"Make sure to moisten the reed for a bit and then, yeah, just let 'er rip!" Ben exclaims.

I follow his instructions, taking a few minutes to moisten the reed. (Side note: Someone really needs to think about inventing flavored reeds. This whole process would be a whole lot less terrible if I got to put a BERRY BLAST reed in my mouth. Just a thought.)

All right then.

I make sure the saxophone is held correctly, attempt to recreate the weird mouth position, breathe in and . . .

SQUEAK!

I am reminded of my Music class embarrassment and immediately put the saxophone back down in my lap.

"That was awesome!" Ben exclaims, and I shoot him a glare. Is he making fun of me?

"No, seriously! It took me a while to even make a noise on the saxophone. That was great, keep going!"

I squeak and squeal my way through the remaining twenty minutes, and Ben says "Good job!" or "You're almost there!" with every terrible note. But even I have to admit that by the end of the session I no longer sound like a combination of screeching cat and nails on a chalkboard. I think I can confidently put myself entirely in the screeching cat category now.

I call that progress.

Ben starts taking his saxophone apart, each piece finding its way into the proper compartment of his case. I follow his lead, and both of our cases fasten at the same time with a "click."

"So just make sure you keep practicing at home, and by next week you'll see a huge improvement. Practicing is the key."

"Yeah, I will. Uh . . . thanks, eh?"

I'm not sure if Ben expects us to shake hands again, so I put my hand in a kind of strange slap/shake position, but Ben just gives me a friendly grin and says, "No problem, see you Tuesday!" as he heads out the door.

You know the phrase, "Don't leave me hanging"? This would be me. Hanging.

But I barely mind the awkward moment. Because, for the first time, it appears that I might just figure out this saxophone thing yet.

JAY   SAXOPHONE

12

CHAPTER 9

I decide to head to my dad's store after school to do some of my homework, and perhaps even try a few more squeaks on the saxophone if the store is empty. I push open the front door and a small jingle from the bell above signals my entrance. My dad bounds into the store from the back room carrying a large stack of maps, which he carefully places beside the cash register when he sees me.

"Perfect timing, Jason. Come help me put some of these maps in the front display, will ya?"

I set down my saxophone case and slide off my backpack, and grab a few of the maps from the front counter.

"How was school today? Did you learn lots of amazing and interesting things that you just can't wait to share with your dear old dad?"

"Oh yeah, Dad, school was absolutely riveting," I respond, my voice dripping with sarcasm.

My dad grins at me. "Well, it was worth a try. At least it's almost the weekend. Any big plans?" he asks as we make our way to the front of the store.

"Tomorrow we have the day off from school, but I have to meet my group to work on our science project, and we have a game on Saturday."

"Is it safe to assume that you will be looking forward to only one out of those two events?" he asks, sticking the first corner of a large map onto a display board in the front window.

"Wow, Dad. You should really think about giving up the map business and trying your hand at being a psychic," I respond, handing him a piece of sticky tack when he puts out his hand.

"What can I say? It's a gift." He finishes fastening the last corner, smooths the surface with his hands, and steps down from his stool. "Well, without being overly sappy, I just want to say that I am very proud of you. I know you've got some added stuff on your plate with the whole saxophone thing and . . . I'm just glad you're giving it an honest go."

"Thanks, Dad. But I'm not sure my 'honest go' is going to be enough to pass my Music test, or not look like a total idiot."

It appears that my dad has stopped listening as he is now rummaging through the pile of maps in front of him, muttering things like, "Now where is that . . . ? I know I had it here somewhere . . ." Sensing our little father-son talk has come to an end, I start to walk toward my backpack when suddenly my father shouts out "AHA!" and holds up a map triumphantly. "I knew I had it. Come look at something for a minute, Jay." I follow him to the counter and he unfolds the map, placing a heavy paperweight on each corner.

"Do you remember that trip we took up north to visit your cousins a few summers ago?"

"Um, let me think . . . thirteen hours in a car with Dylan and Jodie? Yes, I have a vague memory of that trip."

"Okay, so do you remember the route we took to get there?" my dad asks, ignoring the comment about my siblings.

"Yeah, Dad. I mean, you only went over it with us a million times." One thing about having a father that works in a map store is, well, the guy loves maps. Every trip is carefully planned and plotted with a highlighter, and he marks the spots where we'll stop to eat or to see a landmark. Weeks before the trip, my dad shows us, in excruciating detail, our planned route, along with a bunch of other trip information we couldn't possibly need. Approximate stop times. Packing tips. Road trip snack ideas. The list goes on.

"All right, so we started here," my dad begins, tracing the route on the map with his finger, "and we stopped right . . . here. Do you remember what we did?"

I look down at the map. "That's where we stopped to eat, right? At that diner, the one with the big bear in the entrance."

"That's right. Do you remember anything else about that stop?"

"We had to wait forever for our food, so you made a target out of the sugar packs and we took turns using spitballs and straws to try to hit the bull's-eye."

"And then, Dylan . . ."

"His spitball landed right on Mom's face," I burst out, suddenly remembering my mom's death glare accompanying the soggy paper stuck to her forehead.

"I thought your mother was going to kill me right there and then," my dad recalls, laughing. I join in, and when we have sufficiently collected ourselves, my dad looks back at the map and continues following the route upwards.

"And what about here?" He taps on a small red dot.

"That's . . . that's where we stopped to see the goose, right?"

"Good memory, that's right. We all took pictures with the giant goose. Your picture is still hung up in your room somewhere, isn't it?"

"Yeah, it's above my desk." I'm wondering where this trip down nostalgia lane is headed.

"Now, what do you remember about the actual

vacation up north, with your cousins?" He's removing the paperweights and rolling up the map.

"I don't know . . . I mean, we hung out, played together . . . just . . . normal stuff, I guess," I answer, still confused.

"Exactly. When you guys came home you hardly said two words about how you spent your time with your cousins. What you talked about were all the funny things that happened on the way there." My dad puts a bit of Scotch tape on the edge of the map to keep it from unrolling and turns toward me. "Son, some things in life aren't about making it to the destination. Some things are about the journey." He tousles my hair, and walks to the front of the store to finish up his display.

I'm not exactly sure what he means. To be honest with you, half of the things my dad says make little to no sense to me. But for some reason, our talk has made me feel a bit better, knowing that, in his own way, my dad is trying to say that he is on my side.

I finish up my homework, feeling relieved that I will only have my project to work on over the weekend. My dad locks up the store and the two of us walk home for dinner, and I notice that he's wearing a slight grin, possibly still thinking about our trip up north. I find myself thinking about the trip as well, and realize that I'm also smiling.

"What are you thinking about, Jay?" my dad asks, turning to look at me.

"Nothin'," I reply.

"Yeah, me too," he says, still grinning as we reach the walkway to our house.

CHAPTER 10

My dad and I are just hanging up our coats when my mom shouts from the kitchen that dinner is ready.

Let me tell you a few things about dinnertime in the Roberts family.

First of all, my mother, bless her soul, is the WORST COOK IN THE ENTIRE WORLD. I mean, it's bad. It's REALLY bad. There are days when she puts something on your plate and you can't tell what kind of meat it is, or if it's even meat at all. In fact, there are only three things in this world that my mother can cook.

1. Spaghetti.
2. Spaghetti with meat sauce.
3. Spaghetti with meatballs (although, the meatballs are sometimes questionable).

What's even worse is that my mom has no idea she can't cook. She thinks that it's normal to "eat around the burnt parts" and that "sauces are supposed to be lumpy . . . that's how you know they're homemade." So we all have to play along, as though my mom is a gourmet cook, and let me tell you, it is not easy. Usually, when we've had a few particularly terrible meals in a row, my dad will offer to pick up pizza so that he can give my mother "a break from cooking." But we all know it's really an attempt to give our stomachs a break from having to digest yet another questionable, dry, and/or rock-hard meal. (My father has also, on occasion, attempted to make dinner, but the only thing worse than my mom's cooking is my dad's cooking.)

Tonight we are on day three of a seriously bad streak: Mom's "meatloaf" (more like a hockey puck than actual food). I try to push things around on my plate to make it look as though I've eaten more than I actually have.

"There's plenty left in the kitchen, so go grab a second helping if you want," my mom encourages us. I catch Dylan's eye and I can tell he is attempting to hold in a smirk.

"I can't eat this, Mom. I've decided to become a vegetarian," Jodie announces, pushing her plate away from her and crossing her arms. Jodie is always joining a cause, or attempting to make life-altering decisions she thinks will shock my family. We've all grown accustomed to her outbursts, so it doesn't faze us much.

"You do know what a vegetarian is, right?" Dylan says. "It means you can't eat meat. I've seen you stick, like, seven pieces of pepperoni pizza in your mouth in one sitting. It's pretty gross. Come to think of it, I'm feeling sick just picturing it." Dylan makes gagging sounds and puts his his hand over his mouth.

"Honestly, Dylan. Not at the dinner table. Jodie, dear, there's plenty of salad and mashed potatoes in the kitchen as well," my mom says, barely acknowledging Jodie's cause of the week.

"How am I supposed to survive on salad? No one in this family takes me seriously," Jodie grumbles, and she takes her plate to the kitchen, presumably to replace her meatloaf with some leafy greens. I momentarily wonder if becoming a vegetarian would get me out of eating my dinner as well, but this leads me to imagine what concoctions my mother would come up with using meat substitutes, and I decide it's not worth the risk.

"Five bucks says Jodie won't last until tomorrow night," Dylan says as soon as she's out of earshot.

"I'll take that bet. It'll take at least until Monday before she realizes that no one cares," I chime in, shoveling a spoonful of lumpy mashed potatoes into my mouth to look as though I'm making progress.

"Stop it, you two. We need to support each other's decisions and convictions," my mother scolds, just as my father says, "Put me down for Saturday. I was planning on picking up pepperoni pizza on the way home from Jay's game."

"Jon," my mom whispers urgently, which of course sends Dylan and me into fits of laughter.

"I'm just saying, the girl does like her pizza. It's kind of impressive how much she can put back," my dad explains, and I'm pretty sure that even my mom is wearing a faint smile at this point.

"What are you guys laughing about?" Jodie asks, entering the room and sitting back down at the table with a huge mound of salad, obviously trying to make her point.

"Nothing," Dylan says as we all compose ourselves and get back to eating. Or pretending to eat.

There's a moment of silence, and then my dad asks, in his most innocent voice, "So . . . how about pizza for dinner on Saturday?"

Dylan and I start laughing again, and Dad joins in, but one look from my mother and he coughs a little instead. Jodie is rolling her eyes and mumbling something about having to "live with complete Neanderthals" while picking at pieces of lettuce on her plate.

The rest of dinner continues as per usual with my mother reminding us yet again of the extra dinner portions, my father talking about something super boring, and Dylan stretching out his legs so that they hit mine in an attempt to annoy me. When I am finished (and I use the term here not to mean that my dinner has been consumed and that I am full, but finished in the sense that my mother will let me be excused from the table), I grab a granola bar from the cupboard and make my way up to my bedroom.

The rest of my evening consists of doing a whole lot of nothing, which is just fine with me as I have not been doing a whole lot of that lately. By 8:00 I'm already feeling tired, and although 9:00 is supposed to be my bedtime I finally just relent and get into my pajamas. After all, tomorrow I will have to wake up super early for the dreaded group project.

✖ ✖ ✖

Only Kaylee Gifford would make us meet at 9:00 a.m. on a PA Day. (In case they call it something different where you are, PA is for Professional Activity, and a PA Day is a day off school.) Obviously none of us had other plans, like, oh, I don't know . . . SLEEPING? But some kids just don't live by the Kid Code. Now, I know there is not an actual Kid Code, but there are basic rules most of us just instinctively know we aren't supposed to break. For example:

1. Group work should never start before 11:00 a.m. on weekends or PA Days. Obviously.
2. You don't take off another kid's hat, thereby exposing "hat hair."
3. When you encounter another kid back-to-school shopping with his mom, you pretend you don't see each other and never speak of it again. (Especially if you are in the underwear department.)

I mean, it's kind of "Kid 101," but apparently Kaylee missed the memo. Someone really ought to put this stuff into an actual printed handbook for the Kaylees of this world. If you've got some time on your hands, feel free to take on this project. Make sure that Kaylee gets the first copy.

I should have added something to that first rule of the Kid Code. Not only should you not schedule group work before 11:00 a.m. on PA Days, you should also not schedule group work before 11:00 a.m. on PA Days and then be EXTREMELY PERKY AND ANNOYING.

I'm barely managing to keep my eyes open when Luke lightly knocks on Kaylee's door, but that doesn't stop her from babbling away as soon as she opens the door about poster paper and marker tips and other stuff I wouldn't care about even if I were awake. I'm relieved when her mom calls her to grab some snacks from the kitchen, allowing Luke and me to unload our backpacks without Kaylee chirping in our ears.

"I think I'm sleepwalking," Luke groans, rubbing his eyes and then letting himself drop heavily into a chair at the dining-room table.

"If you were sleepwalking, you wouldn't know you were sleepwalking," I point out, pulling the last book from my bag.

GAME TIP #10: *If you are prone to sleepwalking and your sister is having a sleepover at your house, you might want to sleep in something other than your smiley-face underwear. Just saying.*

"I had no idea I was talking to Jay Roberts, sleepwalking expert," Luke mumbles, resting his head on his folded arms and closing his eyes.

"Did someone not get his spinach-and-egg protein shake with fiber powder this morning? 'Cause if you want, I can make a call to your mom and see if she'll bring over a batch for the group," I tease.

This causes Luke's eyes to open halfway, narrowing in on me. "Not in the mood, Jay. Not in the mood." He yawns and has barely closed his eyes again when Kaylee saunters into the dining room with a tray full of food.

"Sweet," Luke says, suddenly fully awake and in a better mood.

"That's for break time. As in, the time we get to have when we have actually accomplished something. If you guys hadn't been so late we probably would have been able to take a break by now," Kaylee scolds. She tries to bat Luke's hand away from the food tray, but he grabs a couple of cookies before she can stop him.

"It's only quarter after nine," I say, looking at the large clock on the wall beside me.

"So you *can* tell time," Kaylee exclaims, putting on a sweet smile and looking in my direction. "See, I thought maybe you didn't know that the big hand should be pointing at the twelve and the little hand should be pointing at the nine. Oh, I'm sorry. Am I going too fast? Do you want to me to explain it *slooowwwweerrr?*"

"Give it a rest, Kaylee," Luke says, wiping a few crumbs from his mouth.

"Where is Max? Why can't people just be responsible and arrive on time? I'm going to go call him. Try not to burn the place down." Kaylee tosses her hair, whips around, and heads out the doorway.

"Max is totally sleeping," I predict.

Luke nods. "We should ... *all* ... be sleeping," he says, talking in between bites of cookie, a few chunks falling out of his mouth.

"You're my best friend, Luke, but sometimes, you seriously gross me out."

Luke grins and swallows his final bite, leaning in slightly. "Did you see who's on the schedule for tomorrow?" His expression has instantly turned serious.

"Oh, you mean the best team in the league? No, I hadn't noticed," I reply sarcastically. The Stars have won, like, five division championships, and one of their players won the league's MVP trophy last year. The last time we played against them we were able to tie it up in the third, but lost by one goal with three minutes to go. I have been eagerly anticipating the opportunity to right that wrong.

"Well, eat a good breakfast, 'cause you'll be up against #8 again. I heard that kid's got an agent and everything," Luke informs me.

"Yeah, right, those are totally rumors . . . you are seriously gullible," I say, pretending that squaring off against the biggest, most skilled player in the league doesn't faze me in the least.

"Awww, is someone afraid of big, bad #8 and taking it out on me?" Luke asks, crumpling a piece of paper in front of him and throwing it in my direction.

"You caught me," I admit, grabbing my own piece of paper and scrunching it into a ball before launching it directly at Luke's head. This, of course, leads to an all-out paper-ball war, with Luke and me seeking shelter behind our chairs, coming up only to launch our ammo.

"Are. You. Kidding. Me?" Kaylee is standing in the doorway, holding a large box of supplies with a horrified look on her face.

"We're doing . . . scientific research," Luke offers, smoothing out a crumpled piece of paper in front of him. "It appears that your, uh, hypothesis about the . . . um . . . aerodynamics of paper is correct, Jay," Luke says, his thumb and index finger rubbing his chin as though he's deep in thought.

"There is something seriously wrong with you two," Kaylee says, shaking her head and placing the box on the table.

Luke and I exchange satisfied grins and pick up the paper balls around us, knowing our little game has come to an end. As Kaylee launches into a breakdown of what we need to get done, my mind is a million miles away, already thinking about tomorrow's game. We might be facing a tough team, but as far as I'm concerned, that's a good thing. A worthy competitor keeps us sharp, keeps us working. And as for their star player, #8? I've got three words for that guy:

Bring it on.

CHAPTER 11

After our group work is done, the rest of my PA Day is spent like most days off from school—hanging out, watching some TV, a bit of shooting practice in the driveway. I decide to bail on watching a late-night movie with Dylan, and the next morning I'm glad I did, because the Stars have brought their A game. (I'm actually not sure they have any other kind of game.)

By the time I come off my first shift we are already down by one, and I'm breathing heavily. I grab my water bottle and take a big swig, trying to concentrate on regulating my breath. It won't be long before I'll be jumping over the boards for another shift, so I need to conserve my energy while I'm on the bench, but I'm still following the play. My coach is calling for everyone to get back, and I see my teammates working hard to get into their defensive positions as the puck makes its way toward our net.

A few shots are taken on goal, but nothing makes it in. Finally, one of our players is able to grab the puck. He chips it long off the side boards and suddenly one of our guys is in the clear—it's a breakaway! Everyone on the bench is up on their feet, yelling and screaming support, although the words are indecipherable in the echo-filled rink. Several players from the Stars are in hot pursuit but none is able to get to my teammate before he takes a shot on net. He goes high to the blocker side, but their goaltender makes a great save. The puck skitters loose from the goalie, who scrambles around the net, clearly in panic mode. A loose puck in front of the net can go either way, and sometimes luck is on your side. The puck slides right back to one of our players in the slot who calmly lifts it over the sprawling goalie.

Our whole team erupts with shouts and whistles, and those of us on the bench lean over the side to drum on the boards with our hands. The Stars' goalie is shaking his head, obviously unhappy, and a couple of his teammates slap his big pads with their sticks, which is hockey talk for, "Don't worry about it, bro."

The celebration doesn't last long. We need to get set up for the face-off.

"Roberts, Howsen, Mitchell," my coach shouts. Bench time is over.

I ease myself over the boards, and as soon as my blades touch the ice I take off toward center ice. The ref is talking to one of the opposing coaches, and a few of us skate around for a few moments until he glides over with the puck. I am taking the face-off, so I am at the red line, bent over slightly with my stick across my knees, waiting for my opponent. When he's finally in front of me, I look up—it's #8. We put our sticks on the ice, both trying to get into the best possible position to win the draw. My eyes, however, are not on my stick. They are on the puck.

The referee drops his arm and blows the whistle, and I keep my eyes on the small black disk that falls from his hands to the ice. I am able to nudge my stick slightly in front at the last minute to win the face-off, and we are now in possession of the puck. But we barely make it past the red line before the other team steals the puck away from us. They immediately begin skating as a five-man unit in the other direction and are at full speed in an instant. One of their forwards takes a shot, and I chase the puck to the boards when it bounces off our goalie's pads. Suddenly #8 is right there beside me, and now the puck is stuck between the boards and the two of us, both of us trying frantically to gain possession.

At last the puck is freed, which allows Luke to scoop it up, and now my team is headed up the ice in full force. The Stars skate back to play defense and one of their players tries to strip the puck from Luke, but he makes one sharp pass before he is slammed into the boards, and now the puck is mine.

Time slows down.

I am skating up the middle of the ice, unable to see Luke in my periphery but I know he's coming up on the right side. My left-winger is already near the net, although he's trying to lose a defenseman who is guarding him closely. As I glide toward the net, I make a mental note about where everyone is located, all the while focusing on any holes where the puck could possibly make its way past the goalie. In hockey, it helps to be strong and skilled and fast, but the best players are also able to see a play develop, to see what is unfolding around them and react accordingly. And that's all mental.

The net is right in front of me but so are two rather large defensemen. One of them comes toward me, but I use a quick shoulder fake, skate around him, and pass the puck to my left-winger, who is now open. He makes a quick one-time return pass right back to me when one of the Stars gets in his face. Another defenseman immediately puts pressure on me, and knowing I don't have a clear shot on goal, I shoot the puck behind the net, hoping Luke will pick it up on the other side. Sure enough, Luke is one step ahead of the defense, grabbing the puck and taking a shot from the right side that the goalie kicks out. A defenseman jumps on the rebound and tries to feed it to their forward on a breakout. I'm in between them and intercept the pass.

What happens next happens quickly and without me even thinking about it. I turn the puck back toward the net, pull back my stick, and shoot with all the energy I can muster. The goalie reaches up with his glove hand and tries to catch it, but the puck sails by and into the net, top shelf ("Where we keep the peanut butter," as Coach says). There's always that delayed moment after the puck goes in, that second where people aren't quite sure if it has, indeed, made it in or not, but once that moment has passed, the rink is suddenly full of noise. A few of my teammates skate toward me, slapping me on the back with their gloves or giving me a quick hug. (If you can call it that—our version of a hug barely lasts a second and we make very little body contact. It's a hockey thing.)

My team has taken the lead, but we are far from controlling the game, and the game is far from over. But hey, we're holding our own, and if we can just keep it coming for the next couple of periods, we might see a victory yet.

We come back to center ice for another face-off, and #8 is in front of me again. He looks me straight in the eyes with an intense expression on his face, and I know exactly what he's thinking, because I am thinking the same thing:

This one's mine.

But this time, it's #8 who is able to push in front, which allows him to win the face-off, and the Stars get control of the puck. We rush back to defend our end of the ice and after some shots on net (a few wide, a couple blocked, nothing that is even close to sticking), the whistle blows. I am momentarily confused. Was there some kind of penalty I missed? I look back at the referee, but he is already making his way through the gate off the ice, along with a few of the players. When I glance up at the scoreboard, I realize that first period is already over. Time flies when you're having fun. And when you're competing with the toughest team in the league, it would seem.

I follow the other players off the ice, anxious to get to the dressing room to adjust my equipment. At some point in the first period my right elbow pad got knocked around, but I couldn't quite get to it without taking off my jersey. Just before reaching the dressing room, I hear someone behind me.

"Hey, #4!" Turning around I see #8 and a couple of his teammates in the hallway.

"That's right, he's talking to you . . . you DO know the number on the back of your jersey, right?" another player chimes in, walking a little closer to where I'm standing.

"Hey, uh . . . nice first period. I just need a second to—"

"Did you like that goal we gave you? We like to do that sometimes, you know, build up your confidence a bit before we absolutely and completely destroy you," #8 is saying, and as he turns around to laugh with one of his teammates I see his last name for the first time. It's Adams. Not only is he one of the best players in the league, but he has an *A* name. The kid probably got maracas or something for his school instrument. Unbelievable.

"See you on the ice," I respond with a cool tone. It's obvious to me that these kids are trying to engage in what is known as Smack Talk. Now, this is all part of the game, and I get that, but I have never really been all that fond of Smack Talk. Mostly because I am very bad at Smack Talk. Let me give you an example of a time I tried to engage in Smack Talk:

Opponent: Hey, #4! Skate much?

Me: (Silence)

Opponent: Seriously, my five-year-old brother's team needs a forward, I can put in a call for ya! And, like . . . you're the right size and everything!

Me: (Silence)

Opponent: Since you can't skate, you'd think you would at least learn how to shoot a puck! See, what you're trying to do is get the puck INTO the net.

Me: Your face looks like my cat.

Opponent: (Looks confused and skates away.)

In my defense, the guy's face did look like the cat we had at the time. It was actually kind of creepy. But, needless to say, Smack Talk is not exactly my forte. For starters, I don't really get the whole Smack Talk thing. A lot of people can talk a big game, but I'd rather do my talking with a hockey stick and puck. Maybe that's just me.

At any rate, all I really want is to adjust my pad before the buzzer goes and we have to get back on the ice. These guys are clearly trying to throw me off my game, but it's going to take a lot more than this. What I need to do is find a way to get out of this hallway before I make a cat comment.

"Everything okay, gentlemen?" I see Stan, one of the referees, walking toward us, taking a sip from an open pop can.

One of the cool things about living in a small town is that you get to know everyone pretty well. And when you play hockey, you get to know everyone involved with the sport even better. Stan has been officiating games for as long as I can remember, and I always feel comfortable stepping on the ice when I see him there. Not only is he a really good ref, but he's just one of those people who's there to make sure everyone has a good time. He skates around from player to player during our warm-up, giving us an encouraging tap on the helmet and telling us to "Have a good one" on the way by. At this moment, I am more than happy to see him, knowing that he won't tolerate any Smack Talk from anyone.

"Of course, sir," Adams says sweetly, shooting me a look and then walking away with his teammates.

"Did you hear the buzzer? It's second period," Stan says to me, taking another swig from his can.

"Already? Listen, I'm starting again this period . . . and I just need to fix my elbow pad," I whine, giving him my best version of puppy-dog eyes.

"All right, all right. Hurry up. I'll make sure they delay it a couple more minutes," Stan assures me.

"Thanks, Stan, you're the best," I say, running into the dressing room.

I quickly pull off my jersey, readjust the pad, and move my arms around to make sure I've fixed the problem. Everything feels comfortable, so I stick my jersey back on and bolt out the door, one arm still being pulled through the sleeve. When I get back into the rink, Stan is talking to my coach, who obviously doesn't even realize I am not on the ice yet, and I slide on, undetected.

The whistle blows. The puck is dropped. Time for us to defend our lead.

CHAPTER 12

I wish I could tell you that we held our lead and I scored two more goals and it was BIGGEST VICTORY IN THE LEAGUE. But in actuality, we tied the Stars 3–3, which wasn't the desired outcome but is still pretty awesome, considering that they're the league champions. Most of all, I was happy that I didn't have to listen to #8 and crew brag about a win. So I'll take the tie for now, but I fully plan on schooling them next time we play. In fact, I look forward to it.

But I'm not thinking about any of that right now. Because today is the very first day of Christmas Break. Let me write that again for effect: CHRISTMAS BREAK. My school project is finished and we actually got an almost-perfect mark on it, so having Kaylee in our group maybe wasn't the worst thing ever after all. (But I will never admit that to the guys. I will deny it to the grave.) I have also successfully made REAL noises out of my saxophone. I know, it might not seem like a big deal, but you forget that I will soon have to play it in front of the whole class, which is still stressing me out, MAJORLY. Anyway, like I said, I don't have to think about any of that right now. I have two weeks off from everything, even from hockey, which kind of sucks, but it's not like I won't still be playing on my own. The point is, I have two weeks to do whatever I want. Two weeks of hanging out, staying up late, and sleeping in. Nothing to worry about. Nothing I have to get done. And when does all of this nonstop fun and relaxation start? Well, my friend, it starts right—

"Kids? Could you come down here for a minute? Your father and I would like to talk you."

—after this. I'm sure it won't take long. Mom is probably going to "lay down the law" about how we need to be in at a reasonable hour and not make a mess of the house and blah blah blah.

My brother and I both come out of our rooms at the same time, and Dylan looks over at me with a raised eyebrow and a slight grin. As is our tradition, we run to the staircase to see who can make it down first. We have been playing this game for years, ever since we realized that our bedroom doors are exactly the same distance from the stairs. So far it has resulted in a broken arm, numerous nosebleeds, a few sprained ankles, and one black eye. But for some reason, not even physical injuries (and certainly not our mom's pleading) discourage us from our ongoing competition.

On this particular occasion, I manage to take the lead for the first couple of stairs, but Dylan grabs my arm and shoves past me. I grab the back of his hoodie to slow him down and try to push my way around, but he blocks me and then puts me in a headlock.

"C'mon, little bro . . . not gonna happen," Dylan says, aggressively rubbing the top of my head, which is a total pet peeve of mine. I struggle to get free, but he's got a good hold on me.

"Dy . . . Dylan, let go. Seriously, I can't breathe. I give up."

He lets me go, a satisfied look on his face, and I put my hand to my neck as if trying to soothe it.

"You are so gullible," I say then, running past him and jumping down the last two steps to our front hallway. Dylan is right behind me and is about to grab me again, but Mom comes around the corner and he stops in his tracks.

"There you two are. Honestly, how long does it take to go down the stairs? And where is Jodie? Jodie? Jodie! I am serious, I want you downstairs right now," my mom says.

Jodie appears at the top of the stairs, holding her hand over her cell phone. "I'm on the phone, Mom! Honestly, can't I just finish one conversation without people interrupting me?"

"I don't know, Jodie. Perhaps I should stop paying your cell phone bill and then there won't be any phone calls for me to interrupt." My mom is crossing her arms with a don't-mess-with-me look.

"Wow . . . you got told, Jodie," Dylan exclaims, laughing.

Jodie rolls her eyes and lets out an exasperated sigh before making her way down the stairs, and the four of us go into the living room, where my dad is sitting.

Wait a minute. Something's not right. Something is terribly, terribly wrong. What is in front of him, is that a . . . a MAP? That can mean only one thing. But they wouldn't. They couldn't be planning a family trip during Christmas Break . . . MY CHRISTMAS BREAK! No, it's not possible. There must be another explanation. Just calm down and let your dad explain that the map in front of him is there because . . .

"We thought we might take a short family vacation during Christmas Break this year!" my dad announces.

NOOOOOOOOOOOOO!!!!!

"A family vacation? What? Where?" Jodie whines, slumping down in her chair.

"Well, we thought we might drive to Indiana on the twenty-sixth to see Auntie Laurel and the boys. We haven't visited them since they moved there, and we thought it might be nice for them to see some family around the holidays," my mom explains, using an annoyingly chipper voice. I suppose she thinks it will make it sound more fun.

"Indiana? How far is Indiana?" Dylan asks, a question that results in a quick, hard punch on the leg from me. You never, EVER ask my dad how far it is to get somewhere. In about a minute flat, he has opened the map and is describing in painstaking detail the route from Parry Sound to Indiana.

Let me give you the short version: it takes eight hours to drive to Indiana.

I can tell by the extensive marking on the map that this trip is as good as done, so I don't even put up a fight. One day after Christmas I will be in a van with my family on the way to Indiana. Do you know what I won't be doing? Having a CHRISTMAS BREAK!

✘ ✘ ✘

We hardly have any time to enjoy our presents since we have to leave on our trip the day after Christmas. I am especially out of luck since my big present was a new hockey net for the driveway (we bought the old one at a garage sale years ago and it's plastic, something for a little kid to play with) and, obviously, it is far from portable.

Our road trip starts out being completely predictable in every way.

Dylan and Jodie fight over where they will sit, Mom keeps pestering us to go to the bathroom (because, apparently, we are all still five years old), and Dad gives us minute-by-minute updates about how long we have until we leave. I'm still packing, which for me means stuffing random items into a bag and hoping I don't forget something important. (Like underwear. Which totally happened once.) I only come out of my room when Dad gives the "five minutes until liftoff" warning. I'm not joking. That is literally what he said.

We pile into the van, Mom finally settling the seating arrangement with some kind of trade-off system, and I put my earbuds in so that I can do some gaming to pass the time. I know I shouldn't get too comfortable, as the inevitable is about to happen. We aren't in the car for even a full hour before it begins.

"All right, Roberts family! You know what time it is!" I can hear my mother even though my game is just about at full volume (she's a loud-talker, remember?) and, unfortunately, I do know what time it is.

Time for ROBERTS FAMILY JEOPARDY.

My mom started this game on one of our first family road trips to help pass the time, and every vacation it gets more and more elaborate. A few years ago she started preplanning her categories on index cards, and then last year she bought battery-operated buzzers so that we can all buzz in our answers. It is, in short, all kinds of ridiculous. But she works so hard on it, and it's not like we're monsters, so we have no choice but to go along. Even Jodie doesn't give attitude about it.

My mom hands us our buzzers, which each light up a different color on this board-thingy that she has programmed them into.

"Okay, a reminder that all the categories relate somehow to our family, and you must answer in the form of a question. The categories are: Past Pets, Fashion Faux Pas, Silly Stories, Hospital Horrors, and Family Member Mania. Jay, since you're the youngest, you get to pick the first category."

"Uh . . . I'll pick, um . . . Past Pets for 200?"

"Excellent choice. This pet escaped from its cage and was never seen again."

BUZZ.

"Green. That's Dylan."

"Who was Hammy the Hamster?"

"That is correct, for 200 points, and it's your board," my mom says.

I am fully aware that Hammy was, in actuality, found a few weeks later in one of the kitchen cupboards. My parents never told me because I took it exceptionally hard when he escaped, and they didn't exactly find him . . . alive. A few years later, Jodie let me in on the family secret, but for some reason I kept pretending I didn't know, and now it seems weird to let the cat out of the bag. Or the hamster out of the cage. You know what I mean.

"I'll take . . . what was the Fashion Fo something?"

"Fashion Faux Pas for 200?"

"Yeah, I'll take that one."

Mom shuffles through her index cards until she gets the right one. "Your father wore these two items together at Jodie's grade eight graduation."

BUZZ.

"That was red. Okay, Jodie?"

"What are sandals and socks?"

"Another correct answer for 200 points," my mom exclaims, turning back toward my dad and flashing him a grin.

"Hey, that is a completely acceptable look. I stand by

my fashion decision," my dad says firmly, but I can see him smiling in the rearview mirror.

My mom shakes her head. "Moving on, Jodie, it's your board."

"I'll do Hospital Horrors for 200."

"Okay, this is what the X-ray showed Jay had swallowed on his third—"

BUZZ. BUZZ.

"That was close, but Dylan had it."

"A Ninja Turtle candle."

"I'm sorry, that is incorrect, Dylan. The next person to buzz in was blue. Jay?"

"WHAT IS a Ninja Turtle candle?"

"That is correct, Jay. You are now on the board."

"C'mon . . . seriously? The stupid question rule? You gave one to Jay last year when he forgot," Dylan argues. "This is totally unfair!"

Here's a funny thing about Roberts Family Jeopardy. It's the lamest, most ridiculous game in the whole world.

But we all still want to WIN the lamest, most ridiculous game in the whole world.

Go figure.

CHAPTER 13

I survive the trip (just barely) and the first month back to school isn't altogether terrible. No group projects, tutoring has been going all right, and by the end of the month I have successfully made more than ONE sound out of the saxophone, but I wouldn't say I'm playing anything that sounds remotely like music. Ben is super nice about my very mediocre (that might still be a nice way of describing my playing) saxophone skills. Fortunately, I did pretty well when we were group-tested in our instrument sections (and by "did pretty well" I mean that I moved my fingers on the keys and pretended to play along).

It's not my fault I'm bad at this. I mean, there's just so much stuff to learn. I don't know if you know anything about music but it's written in its own language. There are all these dots and sticks that go up and down on a bunch of lines, and after you stare at them long enough, they move. I swear! And if you look at them even longer, they spell out things like:

and

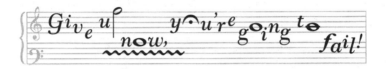

and

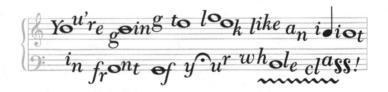

and

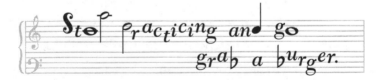

It's enough to make a guy go nuts. Or, at the very least, fail a test. But the fact is, I'm going to have to do this thing, so unless I want to die of embarrassment (that's a real thing), I need to make some major headway. So tonight, I practice.

Just me and my saxophone.

A man and his brass.

A little quality time with the old note machine.

Some one-on-one with . . .

Fine. I'm stalling. You would be too if your mother had complimented you on your "wonderful rendition of 'Happy Birthday.'"

I was playing "Twinkle, Twinkle, Little Star."

GAME TIP #11: *When you are getting ready to blow out the candles on your birthday cake and feel like you have a sneeze coming on, but you're not sure if it's really a sneeze or just one of those feels-like-a-sneeze-but-then-doesn't-come-out-and-just-leaves-your-nose-feeling-kind-of-itchy things . . . play it safe. Turn away from the cake.*

Standing in front of my mirror, I try to remember all the things Ben has been coaching me to do. Hold the instrument correctly. Breathe right. *Ombashoo . . . ombashore . . .* man, I really thought I had that one. I wet the reed (that's right, Kaylee Gifford, Jay Roberts knows what a reed is), take in a deep breath, and blow. A few notes come out, accompanied by a whole lot of squeaks and sputtering. It doesn't sound as terrible as when I started, but it also doesn't sound even close to good. I take a deep breath to get ready to attempt the second line, but suddenly my door bursts open.

"What's up, little bro?" Dylan makes his way over to my bed and plops down.

"Hey, man, ever hear of knocking?" I ask him, annoyed that I am being interrupted.

"No, I haven't," he responds, feigning confusion. "What is this knocking, and how would one go about it?" he continues, leaning in toward me as if expecting an answer.

"You are so funny. Seriously, you should think about leaving my room so you can show everybody just how funny you really are. It would be unfair to the world to waste a gift like that," I say, gesturing toward the door.

"All right, all right, truce. A couple of us are goin' down to the bay for a quick game. You coming, or what?"

"I don't know . . . I mean, I really have to practice—" I start to say.

"C'mon, don't be lame. Perfect conditions out there. Mom already said it's okay."

Now, I really do need to practice the saxophone. I do. But let's say someone were to tell you that you could have a plate of steamed broccoli or a chocolate bar. You should eat the broccoli. You know you should eat the broccoli. Your body even WANTS to eat the broccoli. It would be happy to ingest all the wonderful nutrients and fiber that would come from the broccoli. But here's the simple truth:

Chocolate bar beats broccoli.

And before I can change my mind, I have put away my saxophone and grabbed my hockey gear. For pond hockey, you basically take only three things: a pair of skates, a helmet, and a hockey stick. You don't need any of the padding you wear for regulation games, and my dad says in the "old days" they didn't even wear helmets. That's nuts.

By the time we get to the bay, I realize why Dylan said it would be a quick game. We don't have much daylight left, and we need to move fast to try to get in as much play time as possible. There are only six players including Dylan and me, so we quickly divide into teams and lay a couple of wood stumps on the ice— probably left from someone else's game—to serve as our goalposts. When there are more players we might put someone in to play goalie, but not when it's three-on-three. In this kind of game you're playing just about every position. And when the other team steals the puck and starts skating toward your net, and you need to get back to play defense? Well, then you find out just how fast you can really go.

It's calm, no wind, and I'm happy not to have to fight against that invisible force. We skate effortlessly from end to end, passing the puck between teammates when we need to, shooting the puck when we think we have a shot to make. Without an actual net to stop it, a particularly hard shot can sometimes glide way beyond the markers, so we have to pause and let someone go after it before we can start again.

As I glide up the ice, I can't help thinking that Bobby Orr once played hockey right on this lake. I wonder if he felt the same way I feel about it, like there is nothing else in the world but the feel of the ice beneath your skates and a puck on your stick. I don't know if it's lame or not . . . but I kind of like to think he did.

We play until the puck becomes barely distinguishable on the ice and our eyes are tired of squinting to try to make out our wooden markers. When the game is finished, we take off our skates, tie them together, and put them over our shoulders to walk home. The six of us walk together, each kid stopping when we get to his house with a quick wave or a "Later." Dylan and I have the last house on the route, and after we get in the front door, we say nothing to each other as we take off our coats and boots.

Pond hockey is one of the greatest games on the face of the earth.

And it's also exhausting. I barely manage to put back a peanut butter sandwich and get a bit of homework done before crashing on my bed. I'm asleep the moment my head touches the pillow.

"All right, everyone. The bus has arrived for the field trip, so please put on your outdoor attire and make a single-file line at the door. Please do not bring anything else on the bus with you or it will be confiscated." Mrs. Vanderson is standing in the classroom doorway, looking slightly frantic as she counts a bunch of permission forms while trying to put on her coat.

As I have stated in a previous chapter, Parry Sound does not have a whole lot to offer in the "excitement and action" category. This becomes particularly problematic in the field trip department. One summer, I made friends with a couple of kids who came to Parry Sound on vacation (people actually want to come here for the summer to go "cottaging," which apparently is a thing) and they were telling me all about the amazing field trips at their school. The kid closest to my age went to the Science Center, which is a place, at least according to his description, where you get to stand in giant bubbles and make slime. And his younger sister got to go to a doughnut factory. A DOUGHNUT FACTORY!

But in Parry Sound, there are no science centers or doughnut factories, so we pretty much rotate among three places:

1. The Museum
2. The Water Treatment Facility
3. A nature trail

Today, I have the exciting opportunity to learn about the fascinating world of water purification . . . for the fourth time. I feel like I could probably conduct the tour myself at this point, but I'm not complaining. At least I get out of school for the day.

I tried to petition Mrs. Vanderson to let us go to the Bobby Orr Hall of Fame for our field trip. I wrote a letter and everything:

Dear Mrs. Vanderson,

First of all, I just wanted to let you know how much I have learned in you're class. You always find new and exciting ways to explain things and I for one find it very refreshing. And did you get a new haircut? It really suits you.

Anyways, on a completely unrelated note, I wanted to talk to you about the possibility of visiting the Bobby Orr Hall of Fame for our next field trip. It's not that the Museum and Water Treatment Facility aren't super interesting and there's nothing I love more than an invigorating hike, but I also would enjoy learning more about the GREATEST HOCKEY PLAYER WHO EVER LIVED. I think other kids would like it too.

Sincerely,
Jay Roberts

She responded with this:

Dear Jay,

I am flattered that you find my teaching style such a good match to your ever-growing and inquisitive mind. I do wonder, however, if I was having an off day when I taught you the difference between "your" and "you're." (Please see underlined word in the enclosed photocopy of your letter.) I also appreciated the compliment about the haircut that I received three weeks ago. It is good to know it still looks freshly done.

In regard to school field trips, we do have certain requirements that need to be met in order for them to be approved. The biggest requirement is that the trips need to have some educational component, so that we are not just letting students miss school pointlessly. I would be interested to know what part of a trip to the Bobby Orr Hall of Fame you feel would be educational for our class.

Respectfully yours,
Mrs. Vanderson

P.S. I absolutely love Bobby Orr and have been to his Hall of Fame on many occasions. I even had the opportunity to meet him and have a picture signed a few years ago. It was a real highlight!

Well, now I had to plead my case.

Dear Mrs. Vanderson,

YOU'RE always trying to make everything a learning exercise, even my letter! (See? I do listen. Does that help my case?) There are many things that would *be* educational about going to the Bobby Orr Hall of Fame. For instance:

1. We could use Bobby Orr's stats to make math problems.
2. Using a hockey stick as a unit of mesurement, we could figure out the length and width of different

items. And then we could multiply that together to find the area. (See? I was listening during math class too!)
3. We could research stuff and write a report or something!

YOUR response to this letter would be much appreciated.

Sincerely,
Jay Roberts

The next day I received the following:

Jay,

I should probably just tell you—it's not going to happen. Also, you spelled "measurement" incorrectly.

With warmest regards,
Mrs. Vanderson

So, the Water Treatment Facility it is.

I am on the bus, sitting beside Luke, while Mrs. Vanderson is going through the field trip rules, which no one is really listening to.

"It is a privilege to be able to go and learn outside of the classroom. If anyone tries to take advantage of that privilege, they will be sent home immediately and banned from future trips. Now, the Water Treatment Facility is an excellent place for us to observe and question, but it can also be a place of danger if people are not following instructions. So I want everyone paired up, and you need to make sure you stay with your partner at all times. Both of you will need to stay with the group unless I have given you permission to use the washrooms. Is everybody clear on the rules?"

A couple of kids give a half-hearted "Yes, Mrs. Vanderson," which is apparently good enough for her because she gives a big smile and says, "All right, then! I can feel your minds filling with knowledge as we speak," before sitting down.

"I seriously don't think I have any more room for water purification knowledge," Luke says, turning toward me. "I've heard this speech, like, a million times. I swear I could recite it by heart."

"Yeah, I even know his jokes," I agree. "What did the ocean say to the other ocean?"

"Nothing, they just waved," we both say together before bursting into laughter.

"Seriously, that guy needs new material," Luke says,

and for the rest of the bus ride we discuss the other "highlights" of the water presentation.

When the bus comes to a halt, Mrs. Vanderson stands up with a finger to her lips, indicating that it's time to be quiet. When she is finally able to get everyone settled down, we exit the bus in single file and then quickly find our "buddies." I don't have to find a buddy, because without even asking, Luke and I are partners. It's just one of those things that goes without saying.

My class is led on the tour by a short man with glasses and a mustache named Rick, who, thankfully, is not the guy that cracks all the bad jokes. He is, however, AMAZINGLY boring and keeps losing his place in the presentation, which causes him to repeat just about everything twice. This is awesome, because when there is something that couldn't interest you less in the whole world, it's always better to hear it twice. At the halfway mark, Luke and I do what we always do in the middle of a field trip—ask for a bathroom break.

"Excuse me, Mrs. Vanderson? I really need to go to the bathroom," I say, using my whiniest voice.

"That's interesting, Jay. It seems to me that you had to go to the washroom during our last field trip to this facility. And, if I remember correctly, the field trip before that. I do hope that you don't have some kind of medical condition," Mrs. Vanderson says, a look of false concern on her face. A few kids in the class chuckle.

No matter how old you get in the kid world, talking about bathrooms is still funny. Here are some other things that remain funny:

1. When you see signs that have missing letters or burned-out lights so that they spell different things. Like, it's supposed to say "All you can eat butter chicken" but instead it says "All you can eat butt chicken." That's just good comic material.
2. Rhyming, altering, and/or adding to a kid's name. The weird thing is, most of the names we make for kids aren't all that inventive. But put "Icky" with "Nicki," and something magical happens.
3. People spilling food on themselves or, better yet, getting hit with food. One of the biggest regrets in my life thus far is that I have never been involved in a food fight. Just once, I would love to see someone get a pudding cup poured on their head. I mean, it would be totally hilarious, right? (Unless, of course, that person was me, in which case you could just replace "hilarious" with "horrifying.")

I think I should take this opportunity to say that I DO NOT have a medical condition that makes me have to go to the bathroom (just in case that was unclear). My mid-trip bathroom break is solely for the purpose of getting some time away from Rick and his repetitive ramblings.

"So . . . can I go, Mrs. Vanderson?" I ask, since she has not yet answered my question and is still just looking at me with one eyebrow raised.

"I suppose. Please make it quick, and be sure to take your buddy with you," she replies, turning around to face the rest of the class and Mustache Rick.

Luke and I leave the room and turn left when we get to the end of the hallway. Yes, we know this place well enough to know exactly where the bathroom is. I push open the door and start to comment to Luke how I think Mrs. Vanderson is getting wise to our bathroom scheme, when I stop dead in my tracks.

Leaning up against the wall with Jake, another kid from my class, is Mick Bartlet.

"What the heck are you doing here?" says Luke, beating me to the question.

"I had to take a bathroom break, what does it look like?" Mick responds, folding his arms and giving a sly smile.

"Strange, I didn't hear you ask to go to the bathroom. Jay, do you remember hearing Mick ask to go to the bathroom?" Luke is scratching his head as if trying to remember.

"No, Luke. I can't say that I do. And since only two people are allowed to go to the bathroom at a time, I suppose you two should be running along now," I say, opening the door and motioning for them to leave.

"Hmmmm . . . I think that Jake and I would rather stay. Isn't that right, Jake?"

Jake nods, but I can tell that he would probably rather just go back. He's an okay guy, but pair any kid up with Mick and they suddenly become . . . well . . . Mick-ian.

Mick slaps Jake on the back (by Jake's reaction it must have been a pretty hard slap), steps past Luke, and comes toward me.

"I meant to tell you, that was a really nice goal you had in our last game. I mean, if that goalie had even a tiny bit of skill he would have been able to catch it. You basically just gave it to him."

"Yeah, well . . . I guess I'm lucky that the league has such crappy goaltenders then," I reply, trying to pretend that he's not bothering me and that I am not starting to feel heat building behind my ears. I don't know what it is about Mick Bartlet that gets to me but . . . oh, wait. Yes, yes I do.

HE IS A TERRIBLE, AWFUL PERSON.

Okay, that might be a little harsh. My mom says that when people do mean, horrible things, it's usually because there's an insecurity they are trying to cover up, and that we should never call someone a "bad" person but rather say that they are a person who "acts badly." So, let me rephrase that:

HE ACTS LIKE A TERRIBLE, AWFUL PERSON.

There. That looks about right.

"I mean, personally, I try to shoot the puck using a bit of power, you know, bring some heat. But I suppose, for a squirt like you, it's probably hard for you to shoot like a normal person."

He's trying to get at me. I know this. He knows I hate it when he refers to me as a little squirt, and when people imply that I can't play with the "big boys" because of my size. *He is trying to get you, Jay. Don't react. Don't give him the satisfaction. Just stay calm and be the bigger man. You have nothing to prove to . . .*

"I can outshoot you any day of the week and twice on Sunday," I blurt out, and even as I say it, I wish I could take it back.

Mick bursts out laughing. "Oh you can, can you? I would love to see that. I would REALLY love to see that."

Luke is stepping toward Mick now, and I know what he is going to say before he even opens his mouth.

"He'll prove it. A shootout, you and Jay, 4:00 this afternoon, at the bay. We'll get Brent to goaltend." I shoot him a glare, but he just shrugs his shoulders and looks back at Mick, waiting for his response.

"You and me, Squirt? You actually want to do this?"

No. I actually don't want to do this. It's not that I don't think I can outshoot Mick Bartlet. I mean, he's good, but I feel fairly confident I can take him. But I really don't need this aggravation right now. Also, if he loses, I can see Mick punching me in the face or something.

"I mean, it's okay if you don't want to take me on. I know it's probably *scaywee* for a *wittle* guy like you to go up against a big *scaywee* guy like me—"

"You're on," I hear myself say before I can stop it from coming out.

"Well, won't this be fun! I'll see you at 4:00, loser. You two enjoy your bathroom break," Mick says with a smirk. Then he pushes the door open to leave, with Jake trailing behind.

Luke and I stand there in silence for a moment before Luke finally breaks it.

"I, for one, think it's great to put yourself in healthy, competitive situations that will help to mold and define your character."

"Sometimes you're a real idiot."

"Now, the term 'idiot' in this situation refers to a supportive and loyal friend, right?" Luke grins and points to himself, and I respond sarcastically with, "Yeah, you nailed it," before pushing open the door so we can head back to the group.

At the end of the presentation, we all receive a button that says "Water Works!" and Mrs. Vanderson gives a thank-you speech to Mustache Rick for his interesting and informative presentation. Parents and teachers are always telling us not to lie, but it seems like it's okay when they do it. An interesting double standard.

As we pull out of the Water Treatment Facility, the typical bus-ride antics begin. Throwing things at other kids in the seats farther up and then pretending to look around to see who did it. Standing up and then sitting down as fast as you can before the bus driver and/or teacher can catch you. Waving from the back window at people in cars, and trying to get truck drivers to honk their horns as they pass. It's stupid, I admit, but it passes the time. Preoccupied as I am with thoughts of my shootout with Mick, though, I just can't seem to get into it. I slink down in my seat, shut my eyes, and try not to think about anything at all.

"So, ready to take on Mick?"

Yes, Luke is my best friend. Also, on occasion, the guy drives me NUTS.

CHAPTER 14

"Okay guys, so we're going to do a best out of five. You'll start back here, behind this branch, skate up the ice, and take your shot. Everybody got it?" Max has taken it upon himself to oversee this little after-school competition, and both Mick and I nod to indicate that we understand the rules.

There is an actual net instead of the usual markers so the shootout will be "the real deal," according to Luke. At the edge of the bay, a few of our classmates have come out to watch. (It's more likely that they have nothing better to do, rather than actually being interested in the contest . . . small town, remember?) Mick stretches and then takes a few shots on net as Luke gives me a completely unnecessary and unhelpful pep talk. He's good for that kind of thing.

"All right, it's time to focus. Are you focused?" Luke asks, giving me a slap on the back.

"Uh . . . yes?" I reply, it sounding more like a question.

"Just remember that this is your moment, your destiny. Every minute of your life has led up to this. Fate has brought you here today, to this place . . ."

"I'm pretty sure 'fate' has nothing to do with it. The way I remember it, SOMEONE has a huge mouth, and that person is completely responsible for this entire thing. Who was that guy again? Tall, dark hair, ugly face . . . oh, that's right. It was YOU."

Luke shrugs and gives me a wide grin. "Listen, we can dwell in the past and talk about who got who where, but how will that help you right now? Just focus on your task and try not to think about the fact that everyone will make fun of you for the rest of your life if you lose," he says, and then hands me my stick.

"Wow. As always, super helpful," I respond sarcastically.

"You're welcome!" Luke shouts over his shoulder as he makes his way back to join the spectators.

"Are we doing this or what?" Max asks, looking impatient. Mick and I skate toward him until we are both behind the tree branch. "Coin toss to see who starts. Call it, Mick." Max flips a quarter up in the air and Mick calls out "Heads" before the coin falls to the ice, spinning a few times before it settles.

Heads. Mick goes first.

Mick skates around the ice one time, his hands holding his stick on the back of his shoulders while his upper body twists from side to side. He skates into place, then bolts up the ice with full power and takes a slapshot. But the puck heads straight for the goalie, who grabs it with ease. Brent (who is also the goalie for the Shamrocks) is no slouch. Mick is going to have to do better than that to get one by him.

I stand behind the tree branch and Max drops a puck in front of me. When I see that our goalie is back in place, I grab the puck and start skating toward him. The closer I get, the faster I go, using some of the stick-handling moves I've learned at practice to try to back-hand it in the net. Brent anticipates my move and is able to get his glove on the puck for a save. Not a great start.

Mick is up next, making his way up the ice, and he does a nice little deke before putting it in. He raises his hand up in victory. A few kids whistle and shout in response and he bows before the small crowd. This guy could not be more annoying if he tried. He gives the puck a small tap in my direction so that it lands right by my stick and gives me a small smirk. I take the puck back to the branch thinking about how the only thing I want is to take that smirk off his face.

I start skating, my eyes focused on the net, knowing full well where the puck is simply by feel. Sometimes in practice our coach makes us close our eyes while we do drills for puck control. It's always super frustrating at the time because you know you could probably do better if you could just open your eyes, but in this moment, I am happy for every minute of those drills. I should tell Coach that. Or write him a thank-you note.

Or concentrate on what I am doing RIGHT NOW so I don't lose this thing.

I am seconds away from making my shot, my eyes narrowing at the hole right between the goalie's skate and glove where I know the puck can make it through. I pull back my stick and give a powerful wrist shot that Brent tries—unsuccessfully—to block.

We're tied, 1–1.

I get a few whistles and shouts from the crowd as well, and I notice that Mick is no longer wearing a smirk, although no one would say he looks worried. He skates up toward me and grabs the puck, muttering "Lucky shot" on his way by. Mick's next attempt is a good one, a slapshot that looks as if it might make it in, but Brent makes a sweet save at the last moment, causing me to let out a sigh of relief.

Still tied.

I am able to pull ahead with my next shot. I use the same backhanded move I tried with my first attempt, but when Brent tries to cover it with his glove this time it doesn't work. I don't want to look like I am being showy like Mick, but I can't help but do a small fist-pump at my side, excited to be one up on my opponent. I pass the puck to Mick, who makes no eye contact with me and says nothing. For a big talker, the guy sure seems to get quiet when he's losing. Interesting.

I'm in the lead: 2–1.

Mick skates hard up the ice for his next shot. Using a bit of fancy stickhandling, he attempts to get the puck in the top shelf, but it hits the post with a *clang* and Mick is still behind. He is looking increasingly uneasy, which makes me feel increasingly confident, and that could be why my next shot is completely wide. Like, not even close. You know what they say: "Pride goeth before losing a shootout to Mick Bartlet and becoming the laughingstock of the school for the rest of your life." I'm paraphrasing, of course.

But I'm still ahead, 2–1.

Unfortunately, the next goal belongs to Mick, a shot right down the middle that the goalie is unable to get down in time to block. This seems to bring Mick's spirits up a bit, and he skates over to where our classmates are standing, getting a few slap-fives and fist-bumps. Luke is standing with his arms crossed and gives me a look as if to say, "C'mon, get it together!" and I shrug my shoulders, taking the puck back behind the branch.

We're tied again: 2–2. If I can make this shot, I'll win the shootout.

I try to clear my mind of everything else as I push off to start my journey toward the net. Right, left, right, left. My blades glide one after another in a steady rhythm. The puck feels as if it's part of my stick, moving with it, back and forth, as I draw closer to the target. Brent is bent over, intense and ready. I continue my stride, unsure of what, exactly, the plan is, but in the last few moments I see my opening: it's up top, right over the glove. I pull back my stick and connect with the puck, hard. It's whirling through the air, exactly where I want it to go, but I see the goalie's arm rise and I know that it can be stopped with a glove save.

I watch as the black disk becomes smaller and smaller, whizzing to its destination. It could go either way, into the net, or into Brent's glove—literally an inch from victory or defeat.

I take a deep breath and close my eyes. I can't bear to watch.

Suddenly there is shouting and cheering. I open my eyes and look up to find Brent taking off his gloves and mask. He skates away from the net, and it's then that I notice the tiny, black speck behind him.

My puck is in the net.

Luke is now beside me, talking loudly in my face about not doubting me for a second, and a few of our other classmates have come over to congratulate me. I smile and accept the compliments, but I know there is something I have to do before anything else. I skate over to Mick, who is yelling at Max about unfair advantages, and stick my hand out. If there is anything my parents and coaches have drilled into me it is this: whether you win or lose, you always have to be a good sport. It's not always easy—especially when you've had a particularly crushing defeat, or when you feel your opponents haven't been the picture of good sportsmanship—but you do it anyway.

"Good game," I say, putting out my hand a bit farther so that Mick will see it.

"Yeah, whatever," he replies, but he does shake my hand. Even Mick knows the unwritten rules when it comes to stuff like this. That's just how we play in my town.

Everyone starts to clear off the ice, and as I walk home with Luke, I am more relieved than I am excited about my win. Okay, I'm a little excited. I mean, I should be able to avoid Mick's relentless teasing now for a least a day, a day and a half if I'm lucky. But hey, you take what you can get.

CHAPTER 15

In the next few weeks, I try to avoid getting myself into any more shootouts, because at some point I really do need to practice the saxophone. I think I'm getting better, perhaps good enough to play in front of my mom, but I'm still VERY FAR from being good enough to play in front of an entire class of my friends, and Mrs. Jennings has said that our individual testing will happen in the first week of March. So, like Coach says, "Practice makes perfect." Or, in this case, "Practice could potentially help me not pass out during my Music test."

Once again, I am standing in front of the mirror with my saxophone. (I don't know why I practice in front of a mirror. It's like I want to WATCH myself be embarrassing.) I take a deep breath and start to play. If you were singing along, it would sound something like this:

Twin-kle, Twin-kle, little **BLAR!**

Okay, that was six notes. I mean, it could have been worse. It could have been . . . uh . . . five notes. I take another breath and try again.

Twin-kle, **BLAR!**-kle, little star,

How I **SQUEAK!BLAR!** what you **BLAR!**

By the time I have finished practicing, I have done the song eight times, with fewer squeaks and honks each time. I still can't imagine ever doing this in front of people, but I am at least feeling like I can play my way through the song and it might even be recogniz-able. I would say that's a huge improvement. So I'm counting this one as a point for me:

JAY   SAXOPHONE

Okay, TIME-OUT. This is the part of the story that gets tricky. In order for you to finish this book in any reasonable amount of time, I have to speed through a few things. For instance, you don't want to hear about every single tutoring lesson and practice session I have, right? I mean, imagine if you had to read every terrible detail of my musical life. Not only would that be totally embarrassing for me, but I also feel like the book reviews would say things like:

"A wonderfully humorous tale about one hockey player's musical mishaps . . . until the end. Then it just got seriously boring."
— The New York Times

Now, if this were a movie, I could just show a MONTAGE, which is basically a bunch of video clips of someone doing things over a period of time, set to really cheesy music. Or I could add amazing super-powers and car-chase scenes and special effects and stuff. But we've got what we've got. Work with me here. So, why don't you just imagine me in a series of tutoring sessions that include tears and laughter and a few high-fives. I guess while you imagine me in this montage, you can also imagine a calendar turning from page to page, getting closer to a date with a red circle around it, labeled TEST DAY. And I suppose, if you really want to make this montage thing come to life, you can sing some music while you are picturing all of this, but don't sing anything lame. Also, if you want to throw some of those special effects in there, and a few car-chase scenes, be my guest. The sky is the limit, my friend. Okay, I'll wait for you to finish MONTAGING. (Is that a word? I don't know, but I just used it.)

Okay? All finished? Excellent.

Here is where we end up: THERE IS ONLY ONE DAY LEFT UNTIL TEST DAY.

I have made plans to spend the entire afternoon after school and the whole evening practicing the saxophone. (Wow. There's a sentence I never thought I would say.) As soon as my school day is over, I run home and immediately race up the stairs to my room before anyone even realizes I'm there. For some reason, it is always when I have a million things to do that my parents want me to:

1. Do a random chore. Like sweep the back porch. Why are we sweeping something that's outside? Doesn't nature just sweep things naturally? With wind? It just doesn't seem right to me.
2. Pick up something from the corner store. (Go grab ice? Ummm . . . that's something you can MAKE. It's just frozen water. I can show you how to do it.)
3. Talk about feelings. Every now and again, my parents feel the need to sit down with me and have a really long conversation about my life. During these conversations I am encouraged to

just "open up" and not be afraid to "share what's on your mind." You know what's on my mind, Mom and Dad? How boring this conversation is.

My stealthy escape to my bedroom grants me a few hours to myself so that I can look over my music in peace. I play through my test piece, "Twinkle, Twinkle, Little Star," a few times, and after rendition number three, I notice that it has never sounded exactly the same twice. Is that supposed to happen? Mrs. Jennings did tell us about IMPROVISATION. I guess musicians add in their own notes and rhythm to a music piece, you know, to make it their own Do you think I can pass this off as IMPROVISATION for my test? Yeah, me either.

After about thirty minutes, I decide that at this point there is really no amount of practicing that can save me. I'm either going to do this, or not do it, but staying up all night and stressing about it won't change the outcome. One thing is for sure: I am definitely not looking forward to showcasing my talent (or lack thereof) in front of my entire class. It seems to me that there are really only two possible scenarios:

Best-case scenario: I will stand in front of everyone and completely embarrass myself.

Worst-case scenario: I will stand in front of everyone and completely embarrass myself WHILE failing my test.

I fall asleep realizing that there are actually potential worst-WORST-case scenarios, which mostly consist of the scenarios listed above with added bodily functions.

But no matter what happens tomorrow, I know one thing for sure—it's all on me. Because in a solo music performance, you don't have four other guys to cover you when you're down.

CHAPTER 16

On the way to school, Luke is talking about some new movie he watched, which was something about aliens that can read minds . . . or maybe take over minds. Usually I would be totally into it, but I can't think of anything but my impending doom. You think I'm being dramatic? Well, you've never heard me play the saxophone, have you? It's worse than you think. So, so much worse. Luke doesn't seem to notice that I am preoccupied and keeps telling me about gory scenes from his alien movie, which, by the way, I'm totally going to watch when this whole music thing is done. I nod and laugh and say, "Cool" at the appropriate times, but my mind could not be farther away. I can't believe this day has finally come.

"Ready to rock?"

I jump and turn to look at Luke, but he is looking at me with a puzzled expression. I turn around, and standing behind me is Ben "I like a challenge" Davidson, grinning as usual.

"I'll catch up with you," I say to Luke, and he gives me a little salute and runs up farther to a group of our friends.

"First of all," I say to Ben, "you scared the crap out of me. Second, no, I am not ready to rock. Third, you cannot 'rock' a saxophone."

Ben's smile widens.

"C'mon, Jay! You've been getting so much better. You're going to smoke this test!"

I shrug my shoulders, partly because I don't believe him, partly because I want him to think that it's no big deal and I'm not completely stressed about it.

"Okay, last lesson."

"Ben, I've got, like, five minutes until class and I still have to put all this stuff in my—"

"It'll just take a sec." I sigh and gesture for him to go ahead. "You've learned all the technical things you need to know, but there's one thing that you don't have."

"Talent? A chance?" I probably should have warned you, sometimes I make jokes when I'm feeling nervous. Furthermore, I'm not really good at making jokes.

"No. Confidence. From the moment you started learning the saxophone, you had decided you were not going to be any good at it. And even now, after you've worked so hard, you still won't even consider the possibility that you're not as bad as you think."

Okay, this is a super-cheesy pep talk. I realize this. But I'm also realizing something else, maybe for the first time. Even though Ben and I are VERY different people and I'm still not sure we would ever be best friends . . . I actually kind of like the guy. His weirdness grows on you after awhile, you know?

With this in mind, I try responding a little less snarkily. "I'm not trying to think that way. I just . . . I just don't get it. You know, music."

"Look, I'm going to be honest. You will probably never 'get it' the way you get, say, hockey. But that's not the point. You might never be great at music, or even good—"

"Okay, this is not going in the direction I thought it was going," I interject, suddenly wishing for more of his cheesy pep talk.

"I wasn't finished. You might never be a musical genius, but telling yourself you're terrible at it isn't going to help you NOT be terrible. Whether you realize it or not, confidence has a lot to do with success. Think about when you skate onto the ice. Are you imagining all the ways you're going to embarrass yourself? Of course not. You know that you might miss a shot or make a sloppy pass but, overall, you feel confident that for every bad move you make, you'll make two or three more good moves. So, that's my last lesson. Confidence. Take some confidence into the test today." Ben smiles and gives me a thumbs-up as he walks away. For some reason, I give a thumbs-up in response, but quickly put it down when I realize what I'm doing.

As a side note, here are acceptable kid greetings and/or goodbyes:

1. Fist-bump.
2. Low-five. (High-fives can be acceptable assuming they are not TOO high.)
3. Nod of the chin in the general direction of another kid. (This is usually accompanied by some kind of verbal greeting, such as, "Hey.")

Unacceptable kid greetings and/or goodbyes:

1. Thumbs-up.
2. Handshake.
3. Hug. (I should note that girls find hugs acceptable and hug ALL THE TIME. I should also note that there are specific circumstances in which a guy hug is acceptable, as long as it stays within a reasonable time frame.)

Ben is 2 for 3 . . . let's hope a hug is not in my foreseeable future.

I have to sit through Math and English (I have no idea what happened in either of those classes, and that will probably come back to hurt me later . . . but one failure at a time) before finally making my way down the hall to the music classroom. Mrs. Jennings, who looks extra-colorful this morning, is bounding around, moving music stands for the test. I take my seat, and I'm not sure if I'm nauseous or hungry or have a fever, but my whole body feels like all of those things rolled into one.

Just be confident. I say it to myself, as if that will somehow make it come true. I am just in the finishing stages of putting my saxophone together when Mrs. Jennings claps her hands and puts her finger to her lips the way teachers do when they want silence.

"All right, my little Mozarts! Let us begin our musical testing! We will proceed in alphabetical order . . ."

What do you know about that? I'm going to be one of the last people to play. "Roberts" finally came through.

Each student plays the small selection of music they have been given for the test. There are a couple of squeaks, some false starts, but nothing noteworthy. (Great, now I'm making musical puns.) Finally, I hear Mrs. Jennings call my name, but for some reason, it sounds as if she's saying it in slow motion, like in a movie. You know the kind of slow motion I'm talking about? When someone realizes a building is about to blow up and they shout out to someone else, "Geeeeeeeeet . . . dooooooooooowwwwwwnnn!"

Yeah. Like that. Only replace that with, "Jaaaaaaaaaay . . . Rooooooooobbbbberrrrrrrrrttttttssss."

Of course, in reality, she is calling my name in a completely normal way, and I am just sitting in my seat, staring blankly ahead.

"Jason, dear? Jay? It's your turn." Mrs. Jennings is smiling at me and gesturing for me to come up to the front.

I pick up my saxophone from where it is resting on my case, grab my music with my other hand, and slowly walk up to the empty music stand beside Mrs. Jennings. Everyone is silently staring at me as I unfold my music and place it on the stand. This is it. No more tutoring. No more practicing. It's go time. I think about Ben's pep talk. For some weird reason, Ben thinks I can do this.

Confidence.

I picture myself stepping onto the ice, stick in hand. Of course I'm confident when I'm out there. I know what I'm doing. How to position myself, how to hold my stick, how to control the puck. I can do that. I know I can do that. But then again . . . at the very least, I suppose I do know how to position myself with a saxophone, I think, moving myself until I am holding the instrument just like in my tutoring sessions. And I do know what to do with my mouth to make a proper sound, making the grandpa face I learned from Kaylee.

Putting my lips on the mouthpiece, I suddenly feel as if there is a chance, a slight chance, that I might be able to do this. I blow some air into it, but no sound comes out. I try again, and this time I manage to get out a tiny squeak, barely audible. I look up again. They are all still staring, and I feel that wave of nausea coming back.

I think back to standing on the ice. It's not just that I know what to do there, I realize. I picture myself skating up the ice toward the net, but I'm not alone. My teammates are on either side of me, skating with me, doing their part in the play. It's not just that I know what to do. It's all of us, together, that makes it work.

And suddenly, it dawns on me.

I'm not alone. Ben, Kaylee, my mom and dad, Mrs. Jennings . . . in a way, they're kind of like my . . . musical teammates. Wow, does that read as lame as it sounds in my head? It's possible I am losing oxygen blowing into this thing, so be prepared to call for help if it comes to that. But it's kind of true. In different ways, they've all helped in getting me to this point. I mean, a few months ago, I wouldn't have thought I could even HOLD a saxophone properly, much less actually make a sound out of it, and yet here I am.

I look out at my classmates again, desperately wanting to tell Mrs. Jennings that I don't care if I fail my test, that nothing is worth this kind of embarrassment, that I'm going to leave this terrible classroom and never come back.

But I've never been the type of person to let my team down.

So I try again. This time, I focus on all the things my teammates have taught me. Proper grip. Deep breath. Embouchure. Try my best. Enjoy the journey. (I still don't really get that one, and this journey has not exactly been what I would call "enjoyable," but whatever.) And after a few more squeaks, I'm sorta-kinda-in-the-very-loosest-sense-of-the-word playing. I'm actually playing the saxophone! It's not perfect, it's probably not even good, but it's close enough. I'm pretty sure I finish on the wrong note, but I don't care. I played the saxophone. Did you see me everyone? Cheer for me! Throw flowers at my feet! Hoist me up on your shoulders and shout that I'm number one! I'm number one!

I look up from my music stand so that people can give me the praise that I am due, but no one does or says anything. In fact, barely anyone is even looking at me. The kids in the back row are passing notes, and everyone in the woodwind section is whispering among themselves and giggling occasionally. But you can always count on Mrs. Jennings, who is grinning ear to ear, clapping ferociously, and looks like she might even be a little teary-eyed.

So there's that.

From the look on her face, I feel confident that I am not going to fail my test, and it also appears that I will not be the laughingstock of the school. (Well, not because of the saxophone. There is still a whole bunch of other stuff that I'm terrible at. Look out for the sequel.) As I sit down and put my saxophone into the case, I have to admit that it feels pretty good to accomplish something that I thought was impossible. I mean, don't get me wrong, the saxophone is terrible. And if I ever have to see another saxophone in my entire life it will be too soon. Like, if it wasn't school property, I would run over my saxophone with a car, back up, and then run it over again. All of that being said, I did what I set out to do, and I'm not going to lie, I feel pretty good about it.

A good story should always have some kind of moral in it, like "believe in yourself" or "make your dreams come true" or "work together as a team." I suppose I should leave you with something like that, but even though all of that stuff is true, I'm not really an "inspirational quote" kind of guy. And even though I didn't totally screw up my Music test, I'm not a saxophone guy, either.

"You wanna go out to the bay after school to shoot some pucks?" Luke is asking as I shut my saxophone case.

"Do you even have to ask?" I respond with a smile as we leave the classroom and all of my musical troubles behind.

My name is Jay Roberts, #4.

And I'm a hockey guy.

Final score:

JAY   SAXOPHONE

3   2

Dear Reader,

Although this is meant to be a humorous story, there are three very real truths I hope came across as you read these pages.

First of all, no matter how good you are at something, there will always be other areas in life in which you will struggle. Hockey came fairly naturally to me, while other things did not. A little bit of struggle and conflict is good for a person—it helps to shape their character.

Second, and I believe this very strongly, passion is one of the most important components of life. When you find that "thing" that you are passionate about, hold onto it, and do whatever it takes to keep that passion alive.

Finally, you will meet all different kinds of people in your life. Some will be in your cheering section and some will not. You cannot control how other people treat you, but you can control how you treat other people. Choose to be a person who is respectful, honest, and loyal. When you add those three things together and make them a part of you, they can lead to a lifetime of success.

Bobby Orr

ACKNOWLEDGMENTS

I am extremely grateful to Bobby Orr, for agreeing to let me do this project and for the wonderful afterword he contributed. Thank you for being the gracious, humble man I am proud to have Jay want to follow.

Thank you to my amazing team at Penguin, especially Lynne Missen, who showed great patience with me during this process.

I have many cheerleaders in my life, but none as loud as Gloria Trothen and Michelle Davidson who read my work, even the bad stuff. To the many others in my corner (Sandy Klassen, Sarah Plahcinski, and Kari Loscher, to name a few) your friendship and support is appreciated.

To my incredible siblings, Laura, Erik and Tyler who helped shape this book's content by participating in the craziness that was our childhood. (Once again, Erik—Laura and I are sorry about killing your imaginary friend.)

Many thanks to my parents, Lynne and Vern, for allowing me to be the creative person I needed to be. (Even though at times it drove you crazy, like that time I failed grade 8 history.) Thank you to Pam and Tom Kootstra, my amazing in-laws who have supported this writing idea from day one.

This book would have never been written if it wasn't for my husband, Kyle, who gave me the push I needed. You believe in me, love me and don't make me do laundry. Thank you. Nate and Claire, I think of you with every word I write.

And finally, to God, the giver of every good and perfect gift, including the ideas and words used in this book.